"I Didn't Seduce You Last Night, Chase."

"Who hugged who first?" Chase inquired sarcastically.

"A hug of simple kindness is not a prelude to seduction, my friend," Jude replied in an equally sarcastic tone. "At least, it never was with anyone else."

Chase's eyes were dark and burning, his jaw clenched. "You're making me crazy." His mouth covered hers in a hard kiss of utter possession.

The kiss lasted until Chase raised his head. Jude's lips were wet and trembling. Her breathing was erratic, making her breasts rise and fall. He stared, his gaze roaming from her flushed face to her heaving chest.

"Did…you prove something to yourself?" she asked hoarsely.

"Maybe I did, at that."

Dear Reader,

Readers ask me what *I* think Silhouette Desire is. To me, Desire love stories are sexy, sassy, emotional and dynamic books about the power of love.

I demand variety, and strive to bring you six unique stories each month. These stories might be quite different, but each promises a wonderful love story with a happy ending.

This month, there's something I know you've all been waiting for: the next installment in Joan Hohl's *Big, Bad Wolfe* series, July's *Man of the Month, Wolfe Watching*. Here, undercover cop Eric Wolfe falls hard for a woman who is under suspicion.... Look for more *Big, Bad Wolfe* stories later in 1994.

As for the rest of July, well, things just keep getting hotter, starting with *Nevada Drifter,* a steamy ranch story from Jackie Merritt. And if you like your Desire books fun and sparkling, don't miss Peggy Moreland's delightful *The Baby Doctor.*

As all you "L.A. Law" fans know, there's nothing like a good courtroom drama (I *love* them myself!), so don't miss Doreen Owens Malek's powerful, gripping love story *Above the Law.* Of course, if you'd rather read about single moms trying to get single guys to love them—*and* their kids— don't miss Leslie Davis Guccione's *Major Distractions.*

To complete July we've found a tender, emotional story from a wonderful writer, Modean Moon. The book is titled *The Giving,* and it's a bit different for Silhouette Desire, so please let me know what you think about this very special love story.

So there you have it: drama, romance, humor and suspense, all rolled into six books in one fabulous line—Silhouette Desire. Don't miss any of them.

All the best,

Lucia Macro
Senior Editor

Please address questions and book requests to:
Silhouette Reader Service
U.S.: 3010 Walden Ave., P.O. Box 1325, Buffalo, NY 14269
Canadian: P.O. Box 609, Fort Erie, Ont. L2A 5X3

JACKIE
MERRITT
NEVADA DRIFTER

SILHOUETTE *Desire*®
Published by Silhouette Books
America's Publisher of Contemporary Romance

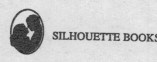

SILHOUETTE BOOKS

ISBN 0-373-05866-7

NEVADA DRIFTER

Copyright © 1994 by Carolyn Joyner

This edition published by arrangement with Harlequin Enterprises B. V.

® and TM are trademarks of Harlequin Enterprises B. V., used under license. Trademarks indicated with ® are registered in the United States Patent and Trademark Office, the Canadian Trade Marks Office and in other countries.

Printed in U.S.A.

Books by Jackie Merritt

Silhouette Desire

Big Sky Country #466
Heartbreak Hotel #551
Babe in the Woods #566
Maggie's Man #587
Ramblin' Man #605
Maverick Heart #622
Sweet on Jessie #642
Mustang Valley #664
The Lady and the Lumberjack #683
Boss Lady #705
Shipwrecked! #721
Black Creek Ranch #740
A Man Like Michael #757
Tennessee Waltz #774
Montana Sky #790
Imitation Love #813
+*Wrangler's Lady* #841
+*Mystery Lady* #849
+*Persistent Lady* #854
Nevada Drifter #866

+Saxon Brothers series

Silhouette Books

Silhouette Summer Sizzlers 1994
"Stranded"

JACKIE MERRITT

and her husband live just outside of Las Vegas, Nevada. An accountant for many years, Jackie has happily traded numbers for words. Next to family, books are her greatest joy. She started writing in 1987 and her efforts paid off in 1988 with the publication of her first novel. When she's not writing or enjoying a good book, Jackie dabbles in watercolor painting and has been known to tickle the ivories in her spare time.

Prologue

Narcotics Detective Chase Sutton stopped his car and narrowed his gaze on the sign nailed to the post at the side of the road.

> Handyman Needed.
> Wages $20 A Day Plus Room And Board.
> Follow Signs To Colter Ranch.
>   Jude Colter

The Colter Ranch was precisely Chase's destination, but he hadn't expected to see any such blatant evidence of someone residing on the place. In fact, from what he considered to be a pretty thorough investigation despite its brevity, Chase had learned that no one had been living at the isolated ranch for several years.

With his hands on the steering wheel, Detective Sutton sat back to ponder this strange turn. Jude Colter had to be involved in the drug shipments; how could anyone live on the

Colter Ranch and not be in on the rotten scheme right up to his eyeballs?

Chase reminded himself that he had no proof of criminal activity at the Colter Ranch, merely a tale from a penny-ante drug pusher who might have said anything to save his own worthless hide.

But the stammered, blurted story regarding a small, private plane delivering heroin to an all but forgotten airstrip on a deserted ranch about a hundred miles out of Reno had brought Chase to this part of Nevada on this sunny Saturday morning, credible or not. He'd taken a few days to do some checking on the status of the Colter spread, and that sign advertising for a handyman was a discordant note among the information he'd thus far gathered. Why would someone neck-deep in the smuggling of illegal substances risk exposure by advertising for hired help?

Frowning, Chase let his gaze sweep the high desert landscape. Sage, bunchgrass and cacti. An occasional lonely tree, a withered, gnarled cottonwood or a scrubby pine. Within his view nothing moved, and his range of vision took in miles of open country. This was back-roads Nevada, unpopulated, secluded, either forlorn or incredibly beautiful depending on one's outlook. This was the Nevada that most visitors to the state never saw, particularly those patrons of the casinos who flew in and, after a few days of fun and games, flew out again.

The distant mountains rose like massive dark giants from gradually ascending foothills. The Colter Ranch was still some miles from Chase's location, but he hesitated to proceed now. Obviously the place wasn't deserted. Obviously he couldn't drive in, find that airstrip and look it over, not with Jude Colter in residence.

Chase looked at the sign again. It was crudely done, black paint on a weathered, unplaned board. After mulling it over for several more minutes, Chase put his car in gear and turned it around. He would retreat for now, but he'd be back.

And he'd be prepared to meet Mr. Jude Colter. Oh, yes, he'd be *well* prepared.

One

Jude felt like her back end was dragging. It was always at this time of day, late afternoon, when she wondered if she hadn't lost her mind. Fixing up the ranch to make it more salable had seemed sound and sensible a few weeks back, but doing so on a shoestring savings account and all by herself was proving to be a lot tougher than she'd thought.

Of course, she never had planned on doing it alone. She had started looking for a hired handyman shortly after settling herself in at the old rundown house. The problem was, with so many mining operations in the general area, no one wanted to work for a measly twenty bucks a day. She felt that her offer of room and board upped the wage considerably, but still, it was understandable why any able-bodied person would reject the low pay.

But it was all she could afford. Actually, even twenty dollars a day for several weeks would put a strain on her limited funds. Ironically, it was her unstable financial situation that had prompted her decision about the ranch.

And so her circle of worries went, one leading to another, until she returned again to the same spot: to repair and renovate what she could, and to sell for the best possible price.

Jude's small knowledge of repairs and maintenance was a liability, which she had been facing with every chore she attempted. Right now, for instance, there was probably as much red paint on her as there was on the chicken coop. There were slivers in her hands despite the cotton work gloves she wore most of the time, her fingernails were a mess, she was sweaty, dirty and discouraged, and the damn coop was only half done.

Jude had hidden her long, auburn hair under a scarf that morning, and was grateful, at least, that it wasn't sticky with paint. She wore cutoffs and a blue knit shirt, and both garments had seen better days. She was ambling, rather slowly, from the chicken coop to the house, barely noticing that the sun was starting to sink behind the mountains in a blaze of color, when she heard a distant sound on the breeze.

Stopping to listen, Jude recognized a motor noise. Something soft and furry rubbed against her ankle, and she glanced down and smiled. "Hi, Biscuit." Bending over, Jude scooped up her cat, which began purring at once. "Sounds like someone's coming, Biscuit. Who do you suppose it is?" Jude let the big cat nuzzle her neck. "Maybe it's someone about the job. Lord, I hope so."

Motor noises weren't plentiful on the isolated ranch. Any vehicle following the gravel and dirt roads from the highway and finally traversing the ranch's quarter-mile driveway could be heard long before coming into view. Occasionally Jude heard what she thought was someone coming, only to be disappointed, so she knew that sounds carried exceedingly well in the valley.

But today she wasn't going to be disappointed. The motor noise kept getting more distinct and was accompanied, Jude realized, by a good many rattles, clanks and metallic groans. The pickup that finally materialized in a cloud of dust explained the unusual groans: it was pulling a horse trailer.

The truck had once been yellow, and maybe, Jude decided with wider eyes, the trailer had once been green. Both vehicles were ancient and rusted. The front bumper on the pickup dangled only an inch from the road on one side, and all four of its fenders seemed to be flapping in the breeze.

"Great balls of fire," Jude whispered, marveling that the shake, rattle and roll contraption ran at all.

Still, she thought with some disgust, that rig looked like it belonged on the Colter Ranch. Certainly it was no more dilapidated than the buildings behind her.

It came to a grinding halt next to Jude's car. The dust began settling and Jude started walking toward the disreputable truck and trailer. The driver's door opened and a tall, lanky fellow with a big grin climbed out.

"Howdy, ma'am."

"Hello," Jude called. The man's jeans were faded from age and wear, as frayed as the old denim cutoffs on her own body. His cowboy boots were scuffed and looked molded to his long, narrow feet. A blue chambray shirt, stretching across broad shoulders and a noticeably masculine chest, had the sleeves rolled up, revealing nicely muscled and tanned forearms.

Chase removed his battered old hat with its jauntily rolled brim. He hadn't expected to see a woman out here, particularly one who was young, pretty in spite of being spattered from head to foot with red paint and, of all things, carrying a huge tan cat. Chase briefly glared through the open window of the pickup and silently cautioned his dog Shorty to behave himself.

Jude came closer and stopped near the front of the pickup. She was having a little trouble with the man's marvelous head of dark hair, which struck her as odd when he was a total stranger and she'd never been one to gawk just because a man was good-looking. But his hair waved in the most intriguing manner, drooping pertly on his forehead above a pair of long-lashed blue eyes. There was at least a day's growth of whiskers on his face, and there was no question that his entire person was rather unkempt. Lord knew, Jude had never been attracted to "unkempt," but there was something about this guy that stirred the female in her.

Biscuit had gotten squirmy for some reason, and Jude adjusted the cat's weight in her arms. "Be still, Biscuit... Something I can do for you?" she queried.

Casually Chase leaned his hips against the front fender of the pickup. "Saw a sign on the highway about Jude Colter needing a handyman. Is he around?"

"I'm Jude."

Startled, Chase stood there—or leaned there—a trifle disoriented. Then he said with studied nonchalance, "Thought Jude would be a man."

The more he looked at Jude Colter, the more female she became. Great legs, a good figure, lean in the right places, curved in the right places. He couldn't see her hair, bound as it was beneath a paint-streaked blue scarf, but her face was striking, with full lips, arched eyebrows and soft brown eyes containing a pleasing twinkle. There was also a note of wariness in their depths, Chase noted, although he didn't know whether to lay it on a natural caution around a strange man or because she had something to hide.

He stood away from the fender abruptly, slapping his hat against his thigh. Jude Colter being a woman didn't change one damn thing. Women smuggled drugs as well as men did.

"Is the job still open?" he asked.

Jude didn't answer immediately. This guy didn't fit the image she'd been carrying in the back of her mind about the sort of man who might come along and apply for the job. She knew now that she'd been thinking of someone older, maybe a retiree who wanted temporary work to supplement his social security.

This guy, who was a little too good-looking, unkempt or not, was in his prime. Around thirty-two, thirty-three, she figured, only a few years older than herself.

And yet he was the only person who had made an appearance; the only one who had shown the slightest interest in the job.

"You can work for twenty a day?" she asked.

Chase caught the suspicion in her voice. "Sign says room and board, too," he stated.

"Yes," Jude concurred. "There's an empty bunkhouse and I'll provide meals. But I have to be honest, mister, I didn't expect someone so...well, young, to apply."

Chase grinned lazily. "Rather have an old handyman?"

"At this point, *any* handyman would look good," Jude replied dryly.

Chase's gaze swept the compound. The place was run-down, to be sure. "What're you trying to do out here?"

"Fix it up to sell. I talked to a Realtor who specializes in ranch properties, and he said I'd get a much better price if the buildings were repaired and painted."

"Then you're not doing any ranching?"

Jude shook her head with a brief, wry laugh. "I don't know the first thing about ranching."

"City gal?" Chase's eyes narrowed slightly.

"Actually, I was born in Nevada. Lived right here until I was five, but..." Jude stopped herself. She enjoyed conversation and lately there hadn't been any, but that was no reason to blurt out her life story to a total stranger.

Besides, she was exhausted, dirty and hungry. "Have you worked as a handyman before?"

Chase stuck his hat on his head, just so he wouldn't have to hang on to it. "Done a little of just about everything, ma'am. Mostly I follow the rodeo circuit. Haven't done too

well lately, I don't like admitting, but facts are facts. I'm
down on my luck and need a job."

"There are much better paying jobs in the area, you
know."

Chase held up a hand, as though warding off something
bad. "Don't mention mines or mining to me, ma'am. Never
did like working with machinery and chemicals." He shook
his head and grinned. "Nope. Ranches are what I like, wide
open spaces and..."

"Paintbrushes?" Jude interjected dryly. From the trailer
came the stamping of hooves. "Your horse travels with you,
apparently."

"Where I go, Thunder goes. Thunder and Shorty."

"Two horses?"

Chase's grin returned. "Heck, Shorty ain't a horse, Miss
Colter. It is Miss, ain't it?" Behind his purposely guileless
expression, Chase wondered if he wasn't laying it on a bit
thick with the *ain'ts*, although Jude Colter seemed to be
taking him at face value.

"It's Miss, but call me Jude."

"I'm Chase Sutton."

They didn't shake hands. Jude's were wrapped around
Biscuit, and Chase thought it best to keep his distance.

"If Shorty's not a horse, what is he?" Jude asked.

Chase turned to the open window. "Shorty! Stick your
nose up there and let the lady get a look at you."

While Jude watched, a dog—apparently a very short-
legged dog—brought his front paws up to the window and
peered out. Jude stared. Never had she seen a less appealing dog. One ear stood up, the other flopped down. His nose
was pugged, his mouth drooped, and the hair or fur or
whatever it was covering his rotund little body was an awful mixture of yellow-and-gray.

"Shorty, meet Miss Jude Colter. Jude, that there fine
animal is Shorty."

Biscuit arched her back in Jude's arms. Shorty yapped and took one big leap over the window frame, landing on the ground in a heap. Biscuit hissed and flew from her perch, hitting the dirt about ten feet away. Jude scrambled after the duo, who were off and running, Shorty going as hard as he could on his four-inch legs, Biscuit well in the lead and heading for the barn.

"Call off your dog," Jude yelled frantically. She had raised Biscuit from a kitten, and the big cat seemed like her only friend at present.

"Heck, that cat could outrun old Shorty any day of the week," Chase drawled. "I'm surprised he didn't hurt himself jumping out the window like that."

Jude turned and glared. "If he harms Biscuit—" Just then Shorty let out a yelp, and Jude whirled to see Sutton's dog making tracks back to his master.

"Looks like Biscuit did the harming," Chase commented with a chuckle. As Shorty ran up, Chase bent over. "Got your nose scratched, didn't you? Maybe that'll teach you not to chase after cats that are twice your size."

Shorty sat down near Chase's boots, panting so hard his tongue was hanging out. Jude regarded the pitiful animal with a sympathetic frown. "He's very…" She couldn't help herself, the word just came out of her mouth. "Ugly."

"Now you done it." Chase sighed.

Jude's gaze snapped from the dog to the man. "I done—*did*—what?"

"Hurt his feelings. He won't eat a bite for the rest of the day. Maybe tomorrow, either." Chase bent over again and rubbed Shorty's ears. "She didn't mean it, Shorty."

Jude was staring. "You're not serious."

Chase straightened his back. "He's a real sensitive animal, ma'am."

"And he understood what I said?" Jude's tone was doubting and slightly incredulous.

"Understands everything," Chase replied in such a positive manner that Jude found herself believing him.

But in the next instant she pulled herself up. "Look, Mr. Sutton..."

"Chase, if you don't mind."

"Chase, then. I was about to say that I'm tired and hungry. If you want the job..." Jude frowned. "Are you sure you want the job? It shouldn't last longer than a few weeks, and I'll expect a lot for my money. I get up early and put in long days. You would have to do the same."

A grin tipped Chase's mouth. "Well, I don't mind telling you that I usually shy away from hard work and long days. But when I put my back to it, I can do a bang-up job. You'll get your money's worth, ma'am, every penny of that twenty a day." His grin broadened. "Let you in on something, okay? I'm looking forward to some home cooking. Don't get much of it traipsing around the country."

Jude nearly laughed. Her cooking would never win any prizes. "Hope you're not disappointed," she said while managing a reasonably friendly smile. "Fine, then. If you want the job, it's yours."

"I want it." Chase hid his elation behind another big grin. It was obvious that Jude Colter was living out here alone. He'd find plenty of time to locate that airstrip and do his snooping. In the interim, it wouldn't hurt him a bit to wield a paintbrush.

Jude turned and pointed. "See that gray building to the left of the barn? That's the bunkhouse. You can park your truck next to it, if you like. I'll get some bedding and supplies from the house while you bring in your things."

Chase nodded. "Is it all right if I put Thunder in the corral?"

"Put Thunder anywhere you like. As you can see, there isn't another animal on the place."

"Except for Biscuit and Shorty," Chase reminded with a chuckle. "Actually, Shorty loves cats. He only chases after them to make friends."

Jude gave him a tell-me-another-one look and thought that Chase Sutton was just a little bit weird.

But he was a typical down-and-out cowboy, looking almost exactly like some she'd seen in Texas. From the condition of his pickup and horse trailer, he might be a little more down-and-out than the norm, but his life-style was his business, not hers.

"See you in a few minutes," she told him as she started for the house.

Chase ordered Shorty back into the truck, which the pudgy little dog managed after a few big jumps that fell short. Then Chase slid behind the wheel and started the motor. He watched Jude go around the back of the house and admired her legs again.

But he banished the thought by reminding himself that he shouldn't be warming to or trusting a woman simply because she had great legs and a pretty face. A frown creased Chase's forehead. His natural instinct didn't categorize Jude Colter as a criminal. Someone had come up with a clever scheme to bring drugs into Nevada, using a little known back door. There had to be more than one person involved—the pilot of the plane, of course, and someone to pick up his illegal cargo. Was Jude the pickup person?

Thinking hard, Chase put the truck in gear and gently released the clutch, giving the vehicle only enough gas to move very slowly through the compound. If Jude Colter was involved, why was she working her pretty behind off to fix up this old place? Why would she want to sell it?

Something didn't add up. Either Jude was completely innocent or damn shrewd.

At the bunkhouse, Chase braked and cut the engine. "This is it, Shorty, our home away from home. Think you can take ranch life for a week or two?"

* * *

Jude bustled around the house gathering up bed linen, towels and bathroom supplies. The bunkhouse was clean and ready for occupancy, being one of her first completed tasks after coming to the ranch. It hadn't occurred to her that finding a hired man would be so difficult, and he would, of course, need a place to stay.

She wasn't altogether thrilled with Mr. Sutton, who struck her as laid-back and lackadaisical as they came. If his vehicles were any measure, he wasn't overly ambitious.

Still, judging anyone by their visible assets was pretty small-minded. Did she have much better? True, her car was practically new and in excellent condition. Paid for, too, for which she had become extremely grateful when the ax fell with very little warning. But what else did she have besides a modest savings account and some furniture back in Texas?

She had worked seven years for a small independent oil company in Texas, only to be told about two months ago, along with thirty-four other longtime employees, that the business was closing its doors. No one understood why. The company had always made good money, which Jude, being one of the accountants at the firm, had known firsthand. It was two weeks later, when she was starting to get very worried because there weren't any available accounting jobs in the immediate area, that she learned the truth: the company had been taken over by one of the oil giants, and their people were physically moving the records and office to their own headquarters.

Some of Jude's fellow employees had wanted to raise a stink about it, calling their discharges everything from prejudice to illegal business practice. She just shook her head and refused to climb into the middle of what seemed to her a brewing fracas that would do nothing but delay her own future, and the unvarnished reality of her situation was that her savings account wouldn't permit a long delay.

Jude was one of those people who rarely bought on credit, which definitely had its positive side: at least she didn't have a stack of monthly payments to face when she was out of a job. By the same token, paying up front for purchases left little available cash to tuck away for a rainy day.

Well, the rainy day had struck, and quite suddenly the Colter family's old ranch in Nevada had become a lot more valuable to Jude. She had contacted a Realtor long-distance, hoping for a fast sale. No such luck. The place was rundown and unattractive. The Realtor's suggestion had been to spend a few bucks for renovations, at least a coat of paint on the buildings.

After thinking about it, she put her furniture in storage, gave up her rented house, packed her car and headed north. During the long trip she had become rather passionate about her "ace in the hole." Seeing the ranch after so many years, and discovering just how badly neglected it really was, had been disheartening.

But she had made her decision and intended to abide by it. Carrying the armload of supplies for Chase Sutton's use, Jude walked down to the bunkhouse, telling herself to be thankful that *anyone* wanted the job.

The building's door was open. "Hello?" she called, waiting outside for a response.

"Come on in," Chase answered from within. He came to the door to meet her. "Hey, you're loaded down. Give me that stuff."

Jude passed the load to Sutton's brawny arms. There were several open boxes and a suitcase on the floor, and she could see that he had already started hanging his clothes on the wall hooks.

"Sorry the place doesn't have a closet," she murmured, noting that Sutton was hatless and that his hair was just as intriguing now as it had been before. Why did his hair fascinate her so much? Suddenly conscious that her own hair was squashed under the scarf, Jude's hands rose to fiddle with the hem of her knit top. She looked a fright, darn it.

"No problem. Those hooks will do just fine." Chase dumped the sheets, towels and supplies on the bed. "Shorty really likes this bunkhouse."

"Shorty does?" Jude looked around and found the fat little dog lying on a rug in a corner, appearing bored and disinterested. "How can you tell?"

Chase shook his head sadly. "He started pouting again the minute you came in. Shorty, Jude didn't mean to hurt your feelings."

"Oh, honestly," Jude scoffed, and turned on her heel. "Supper will be ready in about an hour. There's a gong near the back door. When you hear it, come to the house."

She walked quickly, wondering why fate had sent her a handyman with a peculiar sense of humor. Not that she didn't enjoy a good laugh, but Shorty was an ugly mutt and as dense as a door, and he wasn't pouting because of what she said!

Besides, she was a cat person. Always had been. Jude looked around and called, "Biscuit? Come, Biscuit." At the back door of the house, she tried again. "Biscuit? Here, Biscuit. Come, kitty."

Finally Jude went in without the cat, ripping off the dreadful scarf on her way through the house. She knew, for some unfathomable reason, that she was going to do more than shower and put on clean clothes for supper. Her hair was going to be fixed and it wouldn't hurt to put on a little makeup.

She looked at her reflection in the bathroom mirror and shuddered. "Chase Sutton probably thinks you're uglier than Shorty, and that's saying a lot."

Jude made a wry face at herself. Of course, Sutton would think she was uglier than his dog. He thought Shorty was a fine animal. Wasn't that how he'd introduced the homely mutt?

And besides, why on earth would she put on makeup for a man who probably didn't have two quarters in his jeans? She was lonely, that was all, and Sutton's fabulous hair and sexy body didn't amount to a hill of beans.

Or they wouldn't, if she had one ounce of good sense.

Two

Supper was macaroni and cheese, cold, sliced roast beef—
a leftover from a previous meal—canned peaches, and bread
and butter. There was milk and iced tea to drink; Chase
chose milk and Jude drank tea.

Jude Colter's transformation had Chase gaping, if fur-
tively. Her long, silky hair looked designed for a man's
hands, draping in soft auburn curls around her face and
kissing her shoulders. There was lipstick on her sensuous
mouth, and a trace of pink on her cheeks. Her clothes were
casual and becoming, a floral cotton skirt and blouse, and
pink sandals.

Chase ate and tried hard to appear interested only in what
was on his plate and being shoved into his mouth, but the
woman across the table was giving him ideas of a very im-
practical nature.

Coming to the Colter Ranch had been his idea. He had
discussed the snitch's story with his superior, finally con-
vincing Captain Ryder to let him take a look-see on the de-

partment's time. Then, after Chase had read those roadside signs advertising for a handyman, he'd gone back to the captain with a plan to go undercover and find out what was really happening out here.

Throughout, it had never once occurred to him that Jude Colter might be a woman. Even earlier today, when the two of them had been talking by the pickup, Jude's gender hadn't seemed like any kind of major problem.

Now there was room for doubt in Chase's mind. Jude didn't seem like just another pretty face. There was a quality about her that had him symbolically sweating. An urge to touch her, to do *more* than touch her, had started badgering him the second he'd walked into the house and saw her in a skirt and wearing lipstick.

Chase didn't play around on the department's time. When he was on duty, women were only people to him.

Until now.

His eyes met hers. "Good supper."

Jude took a sip of her cold tea. "It was nothing special, but thanks. I wasn't prepared for another plate on the table tonight." She picked up her fork. "Did you put your horse in the corral?"

"Yeah, Thunder's already feeling at home out there." Chase smiled. "Do you like horses?"

Jude nodded. "I've always enjoyed riding."

"There's a drawl in your speech. Where've you been living?"

"In Texas."

"Thought so. But you lived here until you were five."

Again Jude nodded. Sutton seemed interested in conversation, and she rather enjoyed having someone at the dinner table. "My father died, and my mother took me and went back to her own people. They're gone now. Mom, too."

"And this ranch has been deserted all that time?"

"No. My father and his brother ran the ranch together. Uncle Simon died three years ago. No one's lived here since."

Chase chewed a bite of beef and swallowed. He hadn't known about Uncle Simon's death. "And you inherited the place. It's not a bad place, you know. The land looks good. With the right kind of effort, it could be a producing ranch again."

"Not interested," Jude stated. "I'm an accountant, not a rancher."

Chase grinned. "No kidding?"

"Do you find that amusing?"

"You don't look like any accountant I ever knew."

The admiring spark in Sutton's eyes gave Jude a start, and she brought her gaze down to her plate. "Guess we all have preconceived notions of how certain people should look."

"Yeah, but I'm talking about..." Chase closed his mouth, biting back the compliment. "Well, accounting's a good field, I guess. Don't know much about it."

"What *do* you know about, Mr. Sutton?"

"Chase," he reminded her, setting his fork down and leaning back in his chair. "Guess you're talking about what I might be capable of doing around here, right? Well, I can handle a paintbrush, Jude, and I'm fairly adept with a hammer and saw."

"How about engines? Know anything about mechanics?"

"I can change the oil in your car, if that's what you mean."

"I'm talking about a tractor that won't start."

"Oh, a tractor. Well, I'll be glad to take a look at it. Can't guarantee anything, though."

Jude sighed. She would have to settle for him being a painter and a rough carpenter, which was a whole lot better than what she'd had since starting this project. But her hired man knowing something about balky engines would have been nice.

"Where are you from?" she asked him. Chase had showered, shaved and changed clothes before coming to the house for supper, and his hair had been brushed into a damp, dark submission that Jude found utterly adorable. His clothes were clean but kin to his previous jeans and plain shirt, and he had the most appealing blue eyes she had ever seen on a man. His mouth had a sensuous curve, and there was the faintest hint of a cleft in his strong chin.

She wished, suddenly, that he wasn't just another drifter, a thought that flustered her to the point of nearly knocking over her glass of tea. Righting it abruptly, she waited for his reply.

Chase was wondering how honest he should be, deciding ultimately that there really wasn't any reason for him to fabricate a story in this case.

"I'm from Nevada, the Reno area."

"Then you're at home here."

"Well...I'm in and out of the state," he said without meeting her eyes.

"Following the rodeo circuit," Jude murmured.

Chase grinned. "Yep."

"Sounds like a...lonely way of life." Jude felt a flush creeping into her cheeks. "I'm sorry. How you earn your living is none of my business."

Chase's grin disappeared, and for a moment, while their gazes melded, he felt connected with Jude Colter. "It does sound lonely," he quietly agreed. The grin flashed again. "But I'm used to it."

"I suppose." Jude indicated the bowl of macaroni. "Would you like some more?"

Chase patted his flat stomach. "Thanks, but I'm stuffed." Jude got up and began stacking dishes. "I'd be glad to help," Chase offered, getting up, as well.

"No, thanks. I can manage. Do you give your dog table scraps?"

A twinkle entered Chase's eyes. "Shorty won't eat tonight, Jude."

She sent him an exasperated look. "That's the silliest thing I've ever heard. I don't believe for a minute that Shorty's pouting because I said he was ugly. From the look of his waistline, he eats anything he can cram into his mouth."

"Uh-oh," Chase said, and hurried to the screen door to peer out. "He heard you. He's especially sensitive about his weight. Maybe if you apologized..."

"If I what?"

"He's pretty good about accepting apologies, Jude."

She put her hands on her hips. "This is getting ridiculous. That dog is not insulted because I said he's fat, which is only the God's truth. I'd bet anything that my cat understands more words than Shorty does, and as intelligent as Biscuit is, she only grasps the meaning behind a few human sounds."

"Dogs are much smarter than cats," Chase said calmly.

Jude was getting a little bit angry. "Dogs are *not* smarter than cats. Why would you think such a thing?"

"All right, fine," Chase exclaimed. "You don't believe that Shorty's got hurt feelings. I'll prove it to you. Scrape those leftovers into a bowl or something."

Jude went to a cabinet for a paper plate. "Will this do?"

"That'll do just fine." Chase watched while Jude scraped the little food left on their dishes onto the paper plate and then piled on the remaining macaroni and cheese. She topped the leftovers with a slice of beef, which she was positive Shorty wouldn't be able to resist.

"Dirty pool," Chase said with a grin.

"Give this to him," Jude said triumphantly, holding up the heaping paper plate.

"You give it to him. He might see it as a peace offering and eat it, coming from you."

"He would eat it *whomever* gave it to him," Jude insisted.

"Set it outside, if you're so certain."

Impatient with Chase Sutton's silly game, Jude opened the screen door and flounced outside. Shorty was sitting near the door, and he barely gave her a glance. She placed the plate on the ground.

"Here, Shorty, have a go at it."

Shorty turned his head toward the food, and Jude smiled invitingly. "That's the idea, Shorty, old pal." But the miserable little animal never lifted his hefty hind end off the ground. "Beef, Shorty. Don't you see it? Smell it?"

Jude looked up as Chase came out. "He's just sitting there."

"Told you so. Can't you see the pained expression in his eyes? He's unhappy, Jude, wounded to the quick."

Jude folded her arms. "I don't believe this."

"That's just the way he is," Chase said with unmistakable pride in his pet's integrity. "He's probably dying to be your friend, but he refuses to eat after an insult."

Jude had never seen a dog refuse a piece of meat before, but Sutton's story had to be preposterous. How did a dog know the difference between the words *ugly* and *beautiful*?

She glanced at Shorty's master and suffered another wave of awareness because of Chase's good looks. At the moment he didn't look at all like a transient cowboy. Put city clothes on him, Jude thought, and he would fit any scenario she'd ever witnessed—posh party, business group, or what have you.

She gave her head a shake to clear it. Chase Sutton was exactly as he'd told her, and her wishing that he was more was adolescent.

"It's almost dark," she announced, as though Sutton couldn't see for himself that the sun was down. "I'm going in. Do you have an alarm clock?"

"What time do you want me up in the morning?" Chase was studying his poor unhappy dog with a doleful expression.

"It's light at six."

"Six, then?"

"Come to the house for breakfast at five-thirty," Jude replied.

"I'll be here." Chase hunkered down beside his dog. "Darn, Shorty, won't you take even one little bite? Look at that nice chunk of beef. You love beef." Glancing up at Jude, Chase asked, "Will your cat eat it? Shame to waste that piece of beef."

"Heaven only knows when Biscuit will brave leaving the barn again after being chased like that," Jude said somewhat frostily. "But she prefers fish over beef."

Chase rubbed Shorty's ears, murmuring softly, "Guess Jude ain't gonna apologize, old friend. You're just gonna have to go to bed hungry."

A burst of indignation stiffened Jude's spine. "Good grief! All right. Shorty, I apologize for calling you ugly and fat."

Chase grinned. "Okay!" Shorty leapt up and forward and attacked the plate of food as though he were starving. He gobbled everything so fast, Jude was astounded. In seconds the plate was empty and being pushed along the ground by Shorty's eagerly lapping tongue.

"Is he going to eat the plate, too?" Jude asked coyly.

Straightening, Chase exhibited a pleased smile. "See what an apology can do?"

"Yeah, sure," Jude mumbled, positive that she'd been scammed in some way. "Well...good night."

Chase started to the bunkhouse with Shorty on his heels. Jude was almost through the door when Chase turned.

"Oh, by the way, if you hear anything odd in the night, don't be scared."

"Odd? Like what?"

"Well, Shorty howls sometimes. Only at sirens, though."

"There aren't many sirens out here," Jude remarked.

"No, don't expect there are. Good night. See you in the morning." Chuckling under his breath, Chase continued on to the bunkhouse.

Inside, Jude made quick work of doing the dishes. Darkness had solidly settled in when she was through, and a glance out the kitchen window revealed dim, yellow light coming through the bunkhouse windows.

She stood there, frowning slightly, fully grasping for the first time exactly what she had exposed herself to by hiring a stranger. Chase Sutton didn't seem at all dangerous, if one put aside the potency of his good looks. Surely she had nothing to worry about.

But it was awfully dark out here, and the ranch was miles from the nearest neighbor. In the next instant Jude began worrying about Biscuit. The big cat always slept in the house, and since Shorty's dandy trick of jumping out the pickup window to chase her, she hadn't shown her face.

Jude went outside to call her. "Here, Biscuit. Come, kitty. Here, kitty." She pleaded and called for at least ten minutes, and finally, haughtily, nonchalantly, Biscuit came strolling into the small circle of light cast by the one small bulb near the top of the door.

"Biscuit! Come inside." Jude picked up her cat and hugged her to her chest. Feeling better now that she had her friend with her, Jude hurried inside and bolted the door. After checking the front door and making sure it, too, was securely locked, she put food and fresh water out for Biscuit and then went upstairs to her bedroom.

There was something homey about the dilapidated old house. Jude hadn't spent a lot of time on it, though she had given it a cursory cleaning when she'd first arrived. Painting it, inside and out, was on her list of chores. Actually, painting everything was her main goal, although there were boards here and there that needed hammering into place. Hammering was something Sutton could do much better than she could with her annoying awkwardness around tools, Jude was certain.

The fencing on the place was in bad shape, as well. But she could only do so much, she had decided a week ago, so she would forget that job.

While Jude got ready for bed, she thought of tomorrow's chores, deciding that it would be best for her to finish painting the chicken coop and put Sutton to work on the barn, which was going to be a major undertaking.

As tired as she was, Jude didn't immediately fall asleep. Sutton's presence in the bunkhouse was a distraction she couldn't quite ignore. He was a different kind of man than she'd ever known before. True, he seemed to represent wandering cowboys everywhere, even to his slightly bizarre sense of humor. There seemed to be a laugh behind everything he said, certainly one lurking in the fascinating depths of his marvelous blue eyes.

But those eyes also contained a wealth of intelligence, and in subtle ways belied Sutton's laid-back and careless cowboy image of drawled comments and Western garb. Without understanding the sensation, Jude recognized a pocket of suspicion in her system, a feeling that Chase Sutton didn't allow too many people to really know him.

It occurred to her, out of the blue, that Chase might not function on the right side of the law. Jude stiffened in bed, her heartbeat suddenly quickening. Why would a young, strong man settle for a two-week job with a pitiful salary? Did he choose this back-country ranch because it *was* so far off the beaten path? Maybe the isolation was important to him. Maybe he needed to stay out of sight for a few weeks.

Jude's imagination took her one step further. What if Chase Sutton was on the run from the law?

She groaned and cursed her unthinking haste in putting up signs on public roads without considering the possible consequences. Sutton had a disarming, boyishly appealing grin, but did that make him trustworthy? Everything he owned was obviously on Colter land at the present, his truck and trailer, his clothing, his dog and horse. He lived like a Gypsy, and hadn't she heard all of her life that only roots assured stability? He could be anything, a thief, a con man, a . . . a *murderer!*

Ultimately, sleep separated Jude from reality. But her dreams were chaotic, and she came wide-awake very quickly a few hours later to wonder if that horrible sound had been for real or was merely in her own mind.

But then she heard it again, and she bolted up to a sitting position. What in God's name was that awful caterwauling?

Biscuit jumped up on the bed and meowed, as though asking the same question. The high-pitched howling pierced the air again, and this time Jude knew what it was. Shorty. That miserable little creature was howling, and there probably wasn't a siren within a hundred miles.

Jude tried to get comfortable again, but the howling went on and on. "Damn!" she cried, and threw back the blankets. Snapping on a light, grabbing a robe and sliding her feet into furry slippers, Jude tore from her room and down the stairs.

She fumbled with the back door lock and finally got it unbolted, and she cursed Chase Sutton, who must be sleeping like the dead. Outside, she shrieked into the dark, "Shorty, you idiot. Shut up!"

Another mournful wail was the only response Jude got and, huffing angrily, she stormed into the dark, aiming for the bunkhouse.

The door opened just before she reached it. Chase stepped outside, clad, Jude saw, in a pair of low-slung jeans and nothing else. Her stomach turned over. Moonlight delineated skin and dark hair. She felt his maleness in over-whelming shock waves. His eyes were glittering with reflected moonlight, and she thought he was grinning, but she couldn't be sure.

"Told you he might howl," Chase said from out of the darkness.

"For your information, the nearest siren is probably in Reno. Do something!"

Chase brushed past her, causing a sinking sensation in Jude's body. She caught a drift of his masculine scent and felt her breath catch in her throat.

"Shorty," he yelled. "Thunderation, where in hell are you?"

Nervously Jude pushed the hair back from her face and forced herself to concentrate on why she'd come roaring across the compound after midnight. "How could you sleep through that . . . that caterwauling?"

"Sorry he woke you. Shorty! Get over here!"

And from out of the dark, the little dog came waddling along as innocent as you please, wagging his stub of a tail, actually looking proud of himself. Jude glared at him, barely managing to stifle an urge to call him a lot worse than "ugly" and "fat."

"Obviously he howls at more than sirens," she noted sarcastically.

"I forgot to mention his singing," Chase said calmly.

"His . . . singing?" Jude echoed incredulously.

"Must be a female nearby. He sings to 'em."

"Oh, good grief," Jude groaned. "Now he's a singer. Listen, Sutton, if there's one thing that drives me to the brink, it's having my sleep disrupted for no good reason."

Chase managed to hold back the laughter nearly choking him. "Can't stop romance from flowering, Jude. Shorty's a stud."

"Shorty's an idiot!" She almost said, *And so are you!* But she bit back the cutting words and said instead, frostily, "Please keep him quiet. Five o'clock is only a few hours away, and I'd like to get some more sleep tonight."

"He's sorry he woke you."

Jude cast the dog a dubious glance. "Yes, I can see how sorry he is. He's practically grinning!"

Chase watched her flounce off. Her robe was a pale color in the moonlight, pink, maybe. Her hair bounced with every step, and even in the dark he could detect the female swaying of her hips as she went. He realized, uneasily, that he liked Jude Colter. Not just for her sexy body, either, although that fact was indisputable.

Frowning, almost scowling, Chase went into the bunkhouse. "Come inside, Shorty. You've done enough damage for one night."

In her bedroom again, Jude tossed her robe, kicked off her slippers, turned off the light and climbed into bed. She settled down with a sigh of impatience and determinedly closed her eyes.

But they instantly popped open again, and in her mind was a clear, concise picture of Chase Sutton, half dressed and gorgeous in the moonlight. Him and his damn dog.

Jude didn't have to waste a moment's time in questioning what was going on with her around Chase. The man had a terrific body, probably the best she'd ever seen, and hers was reacting to Sutton's pure, unadulterated sex appeal. This, she didn't need, she thought with sudden exasperation.

Not that she wasn't interested in attracting the opposite sex, but not Sutton, for God's sake. Jude's love life had been limited to only a few men. By choice. Never had she lacked for a date when she wanted one, but she didn't spread her favors around indiscriminately. Sutton was, by his own admission, a down-on-his-luck, traveling rodeo cowboy. This job was merely a brief intermission in his preferred way of life. He probably played along the way with any willing female, and she'd be a damn fool to start anything with him.

Besides, he was weird.

Jude punched her pillow. He *was* weird. Anyone who would label that stupid dog's howls as "singing" had to be weird.

Three

Chase planned to go very easy with the snooping for a day or two. An opportunity would arise, he felt, for him to saddle Thunder and ride out to look for that airstrip. He couldn't believe that it would be any more than a cleared chunk of pasture, but if it was being used, there would be some evidence.

What kept gnawing at him was that Jude—or anyone else who happened to be on the ranch—couldn't possibly miss hearing the landing of a plane. Unless there were some quirky configurations within the ranch's dimensions that muffled sound. He intended to find out.

At exactly five-thirty on the morning after Shorty's mating call, Chase yawned, rapped at the back door of the house and heard, "It's open. Come on in."

Jude was dishing up bowls of oatmeal, and Chase's stomach rebelled at the sight. He hated oatmeal.

"Sit down," Jude told him. "Everything's ready."

Taking the same chair he'd used last night, Chase grabbed for the mug of steaming coffee next to his bowl of dreaded oatmeal, as though the coffee were a lifeline. He wasn't his best in the morning, particularly at this godawful hour.

Unfortunately neither was Jude one of those people who blossomed in the early morning. There wasn't even a hint of a smile in the kitchen, and no one even noticed.

Jude brought a plate of toast to the table and sat down. She picked up the sugar bowl. "This is brown sugar. Do you prefer white on your oatmeal?"

"Brown sugar on oatmeal?"

"Ever try it?"

He took a swallow of his coffee. At least that was good, hot and strong, just the way he liked it. "Think I'll skip the oatmeal, if you don't mind."

Jude leveled an emotionless gaze on her hired hand, who looked just as grumpy and sleepy-eyed as she felt. "Suit yourself, but it's a long time till lunch." She sprinkled a teaspoon of the brown sugar over her cereal and added milk.

"I like eggs in the morning," Chase announced grouch-ily, without a dram of tact.

"So does everyone else," Jude retorted. "But you can't eat eggs every morning and stay healthy."

"My cholesterol's fine," Chase grumbled.

"Well, it won't be if you keep on eating animal fat."

"You eat beef," he countered.

"Very *lean* beef, and not every day."

They fell silent. Chase spread strawberry jam on a piece of toast. He wasn't hungry and had to practically force the food down his throat. His job with the Reno police depart-ment required unusual hours at times, but he'd been work-ing the swing shift for nearly three years and was no longer accustomed to crawling out of a warm bed at five in the morning.

When his mug was empty, he got up and refilled it from the electric pot on the counter. Jude held up her own mug for a refill, murmuring "Thanks" when Chase complied.

With the second cup of coffee, his mind started to come awake. "How big is this ranch?" he asked abruptly, although he already knew that the Colter spread wasn't small.

"Twelve hundred acres. Don't worry, you won't have to see any part of it beyond the compound."

Chase avoided mentioning that he *wanted* to see what was beyond the compound and had every intention of doing so. "You should be able to sell it for a hundred dollars an acre, even with the buildings needing paint. That adds up to a lot of money."

"A hundred and twenty thousand dollars, to be exact," Jude said. "But the buildings are worth something just as they are, and the whole place will sell for double that amount once it's fixed up."

"Is that what that Realtor told you?"

Jude raised an eyebrow. "Do you disagree?"

Chase looked at her. Her hair was free, but another scarf was lying on the counter, obviously in readiness to conceal her glorious mane before she started the day's chores. There was no trace of makeup on her face, and her clothing was similar to yesterday's, old cutoffs and a nondescript blouse. She looked clean and feminine and . . . very young.

"You've tackled quite a job," he commented. "And no, I don't disagree with your Realtor's opinion."

Beneath the table his body was stirring; Jude Colter would make any man think about sex, even at this unholy hour. She had nicely curved breasts and a tiny waist. Her behind was round and firm, and her thighs were the long shapely kind that gave men erotic dreams.

But there was something wrong on the Colter Ranch. Chase believed the snitch's story. At least he believed it enough to check it out, and if a plane was setting down on

Colter land without Jude's knowledge, she had to be a lot denser than she appeared.

Chase's eyes narrowed. "How long have you been living out here?"

His questions were beginning to annoy Jude. She was trying to think ahead for the day, and chitchatting at this time of the morning wasn't particularly appealing in any case.

"That's rather irrelevant, don't you think?" she said with a bit of asperity, and got up to bring her empty bowl to the sink. She turned. "Are you through eating?"

Rising, Chase gulped the last of his coffee. "All through." Had she evaded that question about the length of her residency for a reason?

"There are tools in that small shed." Jude swung around to face the window, intending to point out to Sutton which building she meant, and she wasn't at all prepared for the sudden onslaught of awareness she felt when he came up behind her. Through lips that felt strangely numb, she proceeded with her instructions.

"I'd like you to work on the barn. Some of the stalls are... are rickety. There are missing boards... and such. Everything you'll need to make repairs... is in that shed. Except for lumber... which is stacked behind it."

"I see the shed," Chase said softly, peering around her to see out the window. As though it was the most natural thing in the world for him to do at that moment, he laid his hands on her shoulders.

A jolting desire rocketed through him. He dampened his lips with his tongue and inhaled her clean, soapy smell. His fingers moved on her shoulders without direction from his brain, which seemed to have ceased functioning.

Jude's eyes were wide and staring, but she was seeing nothing. Her lips were parted, and it was suddenly difficult to breathe. A curling heat felt unleashed in her body, moving in pleasurable waves that threatened her grasp on reality. She closed her eyes and saw a startling picture of Chase moving his hands around her to caress her breasts. For a moment she allowed the image to remain, and almost felt his touch on her aching nipples.

But then sanity returned, and along with it, embarrassment. "You can go to work now," she said, her voice low and deep in her throat. "I'll be out in a few minutes."

Chase blinked, as though he'd been off in another world. "Yeah, okay," he mumbled, and let go of her shoulders. Stumbling a little, he made his way to the door. "See you later."

Outside, he gulped a huge breath of fresh morning air in an attempt to clear the sexual haze from his brain. He felt slightly shell-shocked, as though something had shorted out his electrical system.

Shorty was waiting for him. "That lady is lethal," Chase muttered, and the chubby little dog perked up his one straight ear. "Come on, Shorty. Let's go to work."

Jude was still at the window, her stunned gaze following Chase's long-legged stride to the toolshed. Her body ached with remnants of the massive dose of sexual tension to which she had just been exposed. Something very strange had happened when Chase Sutton had laid his hands on her shoulders, something, she suspected, that had shaken him as much as it had her.

She had never before felt so much from simple contact with a man. Laying one's hands on another person's shoulders was an innocuous gesture and should not have caused such intense emotional upheaval.

This arrangement might not work, she worried. Certainly it would be better for her to muddle along with the painting and repairs on her own rather than get personally involved with a man who would be gone before the paint dried.

But the thought of telling Chase Sutton that he was through before he even began created a pain in the vicinity of her rib cage. How would she tell him? What would she say? *You have to leave because you're too sexy* was too ridiculous to consider.

Besides, she was only guessing at Chase's reaction to their brief contact, probably overly exaggerating what he might have felt because of her own foolish palpitations. Whatever he had gotten out of the few startling moments, he certainly hadn't been thinking of anything beyond a quickie fling.

Jude frowned. As worked up as she was, a "quickie fling" sounded pretty darned good. If she went to the door and called him back to the house...? If she invited him upstairs...?

The feverish aches started all over again, alarming Jude. Chase Sutton was the most potent male she'd ever met, but she needed him outside working on the outbuildings, not in her bedroom.

Angrily, uncaringly, she brought dishes and flatware from the table to the sink and dumped them. Grabbing the scarf, she tied it around her head and made sure that every strand of her hair was tucked beneath it. If Chase Sutton had any silly ideas about the two of them, he could forget them; he sure wasn't going to get any encouragement from her.

The toolshed was an interesting place. Chase poked around among the shelves of tools, motors and odd pieces of mechanical and electrical equipment. Everything was layered with a quarter inch of dust, and most items were caked with old grease. It was a musty, airless building that smelled like oil and grease, and from the look of it, no one had disturbed the inventory for years.

Next door was another building, which Chase took a peek into and discovered the tractor Jude had mentioned. He tried the ignition and thought that it probably only needed a new battery, which he would pass on to Jude.

He went back to the toolshed and began gathering up carpentry tools. It was then that he spotted the paint sprayer parked on the floor behind a bunch of old window screens. The thing was as dirty as everything else in the shed, but if he could get it operating, it would make painting that barn, for instance, a hundred times easier.

Chase moved the screens and hunkered down beside the sprayer. He'd seen one similar to it in a body and fender shop the time he'd taken his car in for repairs after a guy had run into it in a parking lot. The sprayer had a long cord wound into a coil, so it ran on electricity. Other than a good cleaning, it might not need any repair, he thought gleefully.

He sensed movement behind him and turned. Jude was standing in the doorway. Instantly he thought of her long legs wrapped around him, and felt her low in his gut. Angry because he couldn't control his damn libido, he muttered a four-letter word under his breath and stood.

"I found a paint sprayer in here," he said almost gruffly.

"Oh?" Jude had only come to the shed to make sure Chase had found the right tools. But electricity had arced from him to her the second they looked at each other, and this time it was *completely* obvious that he wasn't any more thrilled with it than she was, which gave Jude an unsettling start.

"I'm going to plug it in and see if it works," Chase said.

"Do you know how to operate a paint sprayer?" Just why would an unattached cowpoke be uneasy over sexual tension with a woman, hmm?

"I doubt if it takes a genius to operate one," Chase drawled. "The paint goes in this canister—" he pointed at the object "—and is forced through this hose and out this nozzle."

Drawing her thoughts away from their discomfiting personal interaction, Jude lit on the practical. "It would save a lot of time, wouldn't it?"

"And work," Chase added.

"Well, I hope you get it running, but don't put too much time on it. Everything in here's as old as the hills and probably only half of it works. I'm going to get started on the chicken coop. Let me know if you can't find something you need."

Chase gnawed on his bottom lip as Jude disappeared through the door. He knew exactly where to find what he needed, only he didn't dare go for it.

She couldn't be involved in drugs, any more than he could, *less* than he could, he thought angrily. The kind of money that one modest shipment of heroin would bring on the street could buy this place ten times over. She wouldn't be worrying about working her pretty fanny off to double the ranch's value if she had access to that kind of money.

Yet doubt remained, Chase realized with a distressed frown. Until he learned the whole truth about the Colter Ranch and its secret landing strip, he'd be a fool to let down his guard and trust Jude. Who knew what plan might be cooking in the back of her mind? With his present limited information, her selling the ranch if she was involved in airborne drug smuggling wasn't logical, but criminals didn't always behave logically, which was one reason some of the more clever ones stayed one step ahead of the law longer than they should.

He kneeled beside the paint sprayer again, admitting that he'd been here too short a time to be making any kind of judgment about Jude. Only one thing was certain: he'd better keep his damn hands to himself. Fooling around with a woman he might have to end up busting on an extremely serious charge could cause him a lot of sleepless nights in the future.

Jude painted . . . and painted . . . and painted. Her arms ached. Her back ached. Her legs ached. By noon she was seeing red even when she looked at something other than the chicken coop, and she was ravenously hungry.

The paint sprayer had been torn apart and was spread all over the ground near the house. Chase was positive he could get it running, but enough was enough, Jude thought as she dropped her paintbrush into a bucket of water so it wouldn't get dry and tacky while she took a lunch break.

She approached Chase while wiping her hands on a rag. "I'm going in to fix some sandwiches."

"Great," Chase said with genuine enthusiasm. His stomach was empty and growling, and he'd almost reached the point of wishing he had eaten his oatmeal.

"After lunch, I'd like you to pick up this mess and then get to work on the barn."

"It'll be back together in an hour, Jude. It was only clogged with old paint. I've cleaned everything, and I'm pretty sure it will run now."

Jude hesitated. "An hour?"

"Two at the max."

So far, her hired man hadn't done a lick of real work. If he did manage to get that old sprayer operating, though, the time needed to paint everything would shrink substantially.

"All right, two more hours," she conceded. On the way in, she glanced around for Biscuit. Actually, she hadn't seen much of Shorty all morning, either.

But she didn't give two hoots where Shorty might be hanging out, and Biscuit meant the world to her.

"Seen anything of my cat?" she asked Chase, who glanced up and shook his head.

Frowning, Jude continued into the house, suspecting that Shorty had Biscuit treed somewhere, the miserable little hound.

She washed up and went to a kitchen cabinet. There were few decisions to make about lunch. It would be tuna salad sandwiches and canned vegetable soup. Jude sighed. She was hungry enough to eat just about anything, but feeding a man complicated things. Despite hoping for a handyman to come along, her larder just wasn't supplied well enough for imaginative meals. She was going to have to drive the thirty miles to Naples, the nearest town with a grocery store, and load up.

In ten minutes Jude went to the back door. "Lunch is nearly ready."

"I'll go wash up," Chase replied, getting to his feet.

There were black streaks of grease and paint all over him, and still she felt the power of his vivid blue eyes and dark hair. Jude drew an uneven breath. "Fine. Don't be long, though. The soup will get cold."

While she waited, something perverse made her tear the scarf from her hair. She raced up the stairs for a brush and wielded it furiously, and then dashed back downstairs so she would be there when he came in.

The second Chase walked through the door, he smelled tuna fish, which was another of his least favorite foods. He loved fresh fish, but canned tuna had always left him cold.

Still, he was too hungry to worry about what was on the menu. It took him about one minute to make a thick sandwich of tuna and lettuce, which he immediately began wolfing down. The soup was hot and tasty, and he crumbled crackers into it and drank two tall glasses of milk.

Jude was eating with just as much concentration. Never had she noticed an appetite as she'd developed on the ranch. She worked off the calories, she figured, so she wasn't concerned about gaining unwanted weight.

When their first fierce hunger had been appeased, they ate slower and began looking at each other. Jude shaped a tentative smile. "Hope you like tuna."

"Love it," Chase drawled, reaching for two slices of bread to make another sandwich.

"Me, too." Jude's smile became a trifle self-conscious. "I'm sure you've figured out by now that I'm not a great cook. I can do a little better with the right ingredients, though, and I'm planning to drive to Naples in the morning for a grocery order."

Chase's pulse rate increased. Jude being away from the ranch for a few hours would be his opportunity to look for that landing strip. He nodded casually, as though her shopping plans were totally immaterial to him.

Jude got up for the pan of soup and ladled what was left into Chase's bowl. Her generosity brought her very close to him, close enough for her to smell the grease on his clothes.

But underlying that odor was his own; a scent of maleness that affected her clear to her toes. She looked down at his hair and thought about touching it, of running her fingers through it.

She whirled abruptly and brought the empty pan to the sink, stacking it on top of the breakfast dishes she hadn't washed that morning. Resuming her chair at the table, she picked up the remains of her sandwich.

"Jude's an unusual name for a woman," Chase remarked.

"It's really Judith, but I've been called Jude all my life."

"Ever been married?" Chase asked.

Lowering her sandwich, Jude looked directly into his eyes. "No. Have you?"

Chase broke eye contact by dropping his gaze to his bowl of soup. "No."

"Do you have family in Reno?"

"A couple of cousins. My parents are dead, and I never had any brothers or sisters."

"Me, either. I always wanted a brother."

Chase grinned. "Not a sister?"

"A sister, too, but especially a brother."

"How come?"

Jude shrugged. "I'm not really sure, but I envied my friends who had older brothers."

"Your friends probably envied you."

Jude's eyes shot up. "What for?"

Hooking an arm over the corner of his seat back, Chase said softly, "How about for having such beautiful hair?"

He changed the tone of the compliment by grinning. "If I had hair like you, I'd tie it up in a scarf when I painted chicken coops, too."

"Your hair is..." Jude closed her mouth, afraid of where this was leading. She finished almost primly. "You have very nice hair."

Uneasy about the admiration for Jude Colter that refused to stay buried, Chase stood. "Thanks for lunch. Time to get back to that paint sprayer. See you later."

Jude sat there after Chase had gone outside. No matter how diligently—and sensibly—she fought it, her feelings for him were intensifying. She chewed on a thumbnail, stared into space and thought about making love. It was upsetting to be so focused on something that had rarely drawn her attention in the past.

She wanted to fall in love someday. She wanted a husband, a home and children. Someday.

And she had *never* wanted a meaningless affair, but that was what Chase Sutton was making her think about.

Maybe because an affair was all a woman dared hope for from a man like him.

Heaving a sigh, Jude got up from the table and moved to the sink. If she didn't do the dishes now, she'd have an awful batch to wash tonight. The house had an old washer and dryer for laundry, thank goodness, but it wasn't even plumbed for a dishwasher.

Jude meant to take care of the chore quickly, but through the window above the sink, Chase was all too visible, and time and time again she caught herself looking at him instead of at the dishwater.

Who was he, really? Why was he out here working on an ancient paint sprayer, when he could be doing anything he put his mind to? Was he as contented with his carefree lifestyle as he wanted her to believe?

A dangerous thought crept into her head. Didn't the love of a good woman fire ambition in a man?

Jude tossed her head at the foolish fantasy. Any woman who thought she could change a man's nature by luring him into a long-term relationship was asking for heartache, and she already had enough problems to solve, thank you very much!

No, anything with Chase Sutton would be very short-term, indeed.

It was a harsh fact that she had recognized immediately with Chase, but she would be very wise to keep it at the forefront of her mind, particularly those times when she got giddy because he smelled like a man.

Four

The paint sprayer was put back together and functional around three that afternoon. By the same token, Jude had finished painting the chicken coop.

"You should have waited," Chase said teasingly. "I could have done what you did in one-third the time."

Jude didn't care. The coop was finally finished and it looked great. Before starting on its exterior, she had spent two days cleaning its interior, which had been a ghastly job. Now the little building gleamed in comparison to its grubby neighbors. It was, sad to say, the first wholly completed project on the ranch. At that rate, Jude knew she would be painting and cleaning all summer, and she experienced an enormous burst of gratitude for Chase's presence.

Tired but elated, Jude was ready to witness the first practical test of the repaired paint sprayer. "I know the barn needs work before it's painted," Chase told her, "but let's try the sprayer on its broadest side."

"Fine," Jude agreed. She slid the scarf from her head and tucked it into the back pocket of her denim shorts. Tagging along behind Chase, she ran her fingers through her hair to fluff it.

Chase hauled the sprayer down to the barn, located an electrical outlet and plugged in the cord. He opened a new gallon of red paint and dumped about half of it into the canister. Jude watched everything with interest, thinking that if the sprayer really did work, she would have reason to celebrate.

"Ready?" Chase asked with a finger pressed to the On button and the nozzle in his right hand.

"Ready," Jude concurred.

The sprayer motor started chugging and clattering, and a spray of red paint shot out through the nozzle. Chuckling, Chase kept it aimed at the wall of the barn. "It works!" he shouted to be heard above the noisy little engine.

It worked beautifully, and Jude had a smile a mile wide. "Let me try it," she yelled.

Chase passed her the nozzle. "Hang on tight. Don't let it get away from you."

Jude began laughing. It was so easy! The paint came out of the nozzle in a steady stream, and it took only a minute to cover a wide swath.

Just then Biscuit whizzed past right behind Jude. Startled, she took her eyes away from the barn and saw Shorty in a dead run behind the cat. "Shorty!" she screeched. "Stop chasing Biscuit!"

All hell seemed to break loose in the next instant. Jude found herself holding a lifeless nozzle, and puzzled because no paint was coming out of it, she turned to look at the sprayer. But her timing was terrible. The old hose had broken, and the piece still attached to the sprayer was spewing paint. Jude got a face full before Chase could complete his dive for the switch to turn off the power.

Then he made a fatal mistake. He laughed. He not only laughed, he roared.

Furious, Jude grabbed up the gallon can from the ground and gave it a swing, which threw the paint right in Chase's face. "Is it so funny now?" she shrieked.

It was. Chase couldn't stop laughing, even with red paint dribbling down his cheeks. Jude's fury subsided suddenly, and before she realized it, she was laughing just as mindlessly as her hired man.

They collapsed on the ground, although they only laid there a minute before getting up and running to find rags. Still laughing, they wiped away paint.

But Jude's laughter faded when she understood how much was in her hair. "Oh, Lord," she wailed. "How will I ever get it out of my hair?"

"It's water-base paint. Should wash right out, Jude."

"I've got to go in and do it right now," Jude cried, heading for the house. "You'd better shower right away, too. Don't let it dry in your hair."

Jude had a thing about hair, Chase thought as he walked to the bunkhouse. But she was right about not letting the paint dry. He glanced back to the infamous sprayer and chuckled again. Obviously the hose had been rotten and had ruptured under pressure. He could fix that in no time with a new hose, which Jude could pick up at the Naples hardware store when she shopped for groceries in the morning.

Jude shampooed her hair four times. The shower water ran red until the fourth scrubbing, and she finally stepped out of the stall paint-free. She dried off and thought about the incident with mixed emotions. It had been funny, but Chase shouldn't have laughed. She wasn't proud of losing her temper and dousing him with paint, but in a way it had served him right.

At her bedroom closet she debated about what to put on. Was it too late in the day to start working on another building? Chase was obviously more mechanically minded than he'd said. Maybe they should discuss project priority. He could probably repair the sprayer hose and save them both a tremendous amount of hard labor.

In the end, deciding that there would be no more painting today, Jude yanked on a pair of her better jeans and a blue silk blouse. She combed her wet hair back from her face and applied a little makeup. Then she went downstairs to the kitchen to see what she could scare up for supper.

She was still searching the cabinets for something good when Chase rapped at the door, calling, "Everything okay with you, Jude?"

"I'm fine. Come on in."

"Stay, Shorty," Chase said to his dog before entering the house. He grinned when he saw Jude, looking as shiny clean as a new penny. "You got off all the paint. Me, too."

Jude's smile was rather sheepish. "Sorry I threw the rest of that paint at you. It wasn't your fault the hose broke."

"Sorry I laughed."

They smiled at each other, then began talking at the same time.

"What do you want me to—?"

"I was just looking in the cupboards for—"

Chase stopped. "Go ahead. What were you saying?"

"No, you first," Jude insisted.

"Well, seeing as how the day's almost gone, I was wondering if you want me to get started on the barn or do something else."

"Maybe we should talk about that. Do you think you can fix the sprayer again?"

"It only needs a new hose. You should be able to get one at the hardware store when you go to Naples in the morning."

Jude frowned slightly. "Will it cost very much?"

"Under twenty dollars, I'd say. That's only a guess, but it shouldn't cost much more than that."

"Good," Jude said, her expression clearing.

The speculation about Jude Colter in Chase's mind took another turn. If she was part of a drug-smuggling ring, she wouldn't be this short of money.

His eyes narrowed. "Is money a problem, Jude?"

Jude thought her financial situation had to be perfectly obvious. Why else would she offer such paltry wages to a handyman? For that matter, why else would she be doing the work out here at all? If money wasn't a problem, she would hire an army of professionals and have the place looking like a photo out of *Country Living* magazine in no time.

But admitting to a man she barely knew that she was struggling with nickels when she needed dollars wasn't her style. Money had always been a private subject to the Colters, certainly to her mother, who had died almost penniless and not one person in Hastings, Texas, had even suspected. Jude herself had been surprised by the small amount in her mother's bank account when she'd finally been given access to it.

She told Chase an out-and-out lie to avoid the truth. After all, he wouldn't be around to ever know it was a lie. "I'm a little short, temporarily. I'll be coming into some money in the near future."

"When the ranch sells," Chase said, almost holding his breath with a sudden sharp dread.

"Oh, no," Jude said reassuringly, because anyone with a lick of sense wouldn't try to predict how fast a piece of property might sell. Particularly this kind of out-of-the-way property. "Something else."

She couldn't have said anything that would have hit Chase any harder. His stomach knotted, and it took all of his self-control not to clench his fists.

His voice cooled considerably. "Which will it be, the barn or something else?"

"What? Oh, the barn will be fine." Jude offered a smile. "I'm going to start supper early. Listen for the gong, all right?"

"Yeah, okay," Chase muttered, and left the kitchen so abruptly Jude followed him to the screen door and watched with a puzzled frown as he strode across the compound toward the barn. Waddling furiously, Shorty tried to keep up.

Their brief conversation about money had upset Chase in some strange way, Jude realized uneasily. She shouldn't have lied. Damn it, she hated lies, but why would he ask her if money was a problem? Near strangers didn't discuss such personal matters.

When Chase disappeared into the barn, Jude turned away from the screen door. She still didn't know what to make for supper, but it didn't seem so important now. Chase's disapproval, or annoyance, or whatever it was that had stolen his grin, had all but destroyed her previous enthusiasm for putting a decent meal on the table.

Chase had deliberately altered his mood and was grinning again when he came in for supper. Letting his emotions escape with a suspect was unprofessional... and foolhardy. What hurt was that Jude had put herself back into the "suspect" category. He'd been leaning the other way, leaning *far* the other way, having nearly convinced himself that Jude couldn't possibly be mixed up in anything criminal.

He ate her so-so casserole of chicken and rice, and her really peculiar-tasting dish of zucchini, carrots and cabbage, a combination he'd never even heard of, and tried to think of ways to steer the conversation to that airstrip without making her suspicious.

"Thought I heard a small plane this afternoon," he commented after a swallow of coffee. Jude did make great coffee. "Flying real low, as though it was going to land."

NEVADA DRIFTER   55

Jude's eyes lifted. "Really? Maybe it was a spray plane. Some ranchers have their fields sprayed by small planes."

"Could've been, I guess."

"How far did you get on the barn?"

He told her, and they discussed loose boards and barn stalls for a while.

"I spent a few minutes at the corral with Thunder," Jude said. "He's a beauty, Chase. How long have you owned him?"

"Three years."

Jude thought of asking if he ever let anyone else ride his horse, but it seemed terribly presumptuous so she didn't mention it.

"What events do you enter in rodeo?" she asked next.

The question caught Chase unprepared. "Uh, bull-riding, mostly. Some bareback. Do you like rodeo?" he questioned quickly.

"Love rodeo. Been a while since I've attended one, though." Jude's face lit up suddenly. "Say, didn't I see a poster in Naples about a rodeo coming up? Yes, I'm sure I did. Are you planning to enter?"

"Uh, can't. Hurt my back a few weeks ago. Landed hard. Fell wrong."

"You hurt your back? Should you be doing physical labor?"

Chase groaned inwardly. Jude was getting in a hell of a lot more questions than he was, and if she had the slightest inclination to doubt his answers, she would figure out in two shakes that he wasn't a rodeo cowboy.

"My back's fine for ordinary work. Just can't do a lot of riding for...a month or so." Chase managed a grin. "Doctor's orders."

How odd that he hadn't said anything about his doctor's orders when he'd applied for the job, Jude thought. Unless he was afraid she wouldn't hire a man with a bad back.

Her heart softened. He really needed this job. Many proud men were reluctant to admit an infirmity, a bit of masculine foolishness when one's health was at stake. But men were such children sometimes. Chase's pride was rather endearing, actually.

And looking at him across the table was pure pleasure. Jude loved looking at him. He'd gotten some sun today and his color was higher than it had been yesterday. His eyes were so blue they seemed to glow and, like last night, his marvelous hair was damp and brushed down close to his head. Jude knew now that the minute Chase's hair dried, it sprang back into its own disorderly pattern.

She thought of last night and smiled broadly. "Will Shorty eat tonight?"

Chase laughed softly. "I'm sure he will, but tonight he'll be eating his dog food."

"No leftovers at all?"

Leaning forward, Chase dropped his voice to a near whisper. "I don't want him to hear this, but you were right when you called him fat. The vet put him on a low-fat diet, and you should have heard the howl Shorty put up. He hates that vet with a passion."

Resting her elbow on the table, Jude put her chin in her hand. "I'm fascinated, but you're so full of baloney it's a wonder it's not coming out of your ears."

She looked so pretty sitting there with that spoofing expression, Chase forgot all about suspecting her of any wrongdoing and thought again of charming her into bed. It wouldn't be hard to do if that sweet female look in her big brown eyes was any measure.

Their gazes locked. Neither moved. Chase murmured softly, "You think I'm full of baloney, huh?"

Jude licked her lips, slowly. "Aren't you?"

"You're mighty pretty, you know."

She swallowed. "Am I?"

"And full of questions."

"Better than baloney... maybe."

The electrically charged moment passed when Chase grinned. "Yeah, maybe."

Jude stole a silent but much needed breath. Her heart was pounding, and she picked up her glass for a healthy swallow of tea to dampen her dry mouth. Chase's career, or lack thereof, was losing importance, which should scare the living daylights out of her. Did she want a roaming cowboy as a permanent—or rather, transitory—fixture in her life? What was wrong with her? Wasn't her life already unstable enough without adding that unnecessary complication?

Again Chase offered to help with the dishes, and again Jude refused with thanks. Only her voice wasn't altogether steady when she spoke, and after he had gone, she sank back onto her chair at the table and unhappily stared at a wall.

Chase wasn't any happier in the bunkhouse. He paced the floor, raked his hair into a mess, and cursed under his breath, simply because every cell in his desire-racked body was telling him to return to the house and take Jude in his arms, kiss her soft, full lips, run his fingers through her hair and...

The "ands" went on and on. His imagination wouldn't quit, taking him clear to the bedroom. This—whatever "this" was—was happening much too fast and without his consent. It had to stop. He had to remember who she was, or who she could be. Losing control of his stupid tongue— telling her she was pretty was going way out on a limb—and then coming down here to walk the floor because he was horny was ridiculous!

He fed Shorty and ignored his pet's sorrowful look when there was only dog food in his dish. Then he undressed, got into bed, turned out the light and punched the hell out of his pillow.

At the house, Jude did the dishes with a sullen pout. Life was the pits sometimes. When the kitchen was tidy, she went outside and called Biscuit, and then scolded the cat when she finally deigned to make an appearance.

The Colter Ranch was silent and dark very early. Jude lay in her bed and thought about Chase, and he lay in his and thought about her. Both of them, for their own reasons, knew they were dealing with forbidden fruit.

Recognizing the danger didn't stop the craving.

Jude left for Naples at eight the next morning. Breakfast had been a silent affair, but the lack of communication had only been because both Jude and Chase were so grumpy in the morning. The sizzle from last night was still present, not as pronounced as it had been then, but strong enough that Jude avoided looking directly at her hired man.

"Keep on with the barn while I'm gone," she told him. "I should be back in a few hours."

"Take your time."

The minute Jude's car was out of sight, Chase ceased all work and saddled Thunder. The big bay was prancing and eager for exercise, but Chase swung up into the saddle with a grim expression. Thunder was usually boarded at a friend's small ranchette just outside of Reno. It was rare when Chase and his horse had this amount of land to roam, and ordinarily the prospect would have been thrilling. Today Chase didn't feel at all thrilled; should he find the right sort of evidence on the Colter Ranch, he would be putting Jude under arrest.

Urging Thunder into a canter, Chase headed for a bank of rolling hills. Somewhere in those hills, he suspected, was that airstrip, not visible from the compound, perhaps not even audible.

But he was positive of one thing: Jude hadn't yet gone anywhere at night. He might not have heard a small plane land on a distant airstrip, but he never would have missed a car engine right under his nose.

Chase wasn't keeping track of time, though he wouldn't dawdle. But this could be his only opportunity to ride off without a dozen questions from Jude and he had to make the most of it. If she got back before he did, he'd think of something to explain why he was out riding instead of working.

He directed Thunder through clumps of sage, noting that any cattle and horse droppings were years old. There were old dirt roads crisscrossing the land, following fence lines, that hadn't been used in ages.

Then he began to see the land for its own worth. The air was warm but with that high-country tang of freshness that kept summer temperatures pleasant in northern Nevada. It was pretty out here, Chase thought, beautiful, in fact. And quiet, peaceful. The only sounds were Thunder's hooves on the ground and the various songs and trills of birds.

Chase glanced back. The ranch buildings appeared small and nicely arranged from this distance. A man could make something out of this place, if he was so inclined. It would take work, make no mistake. The fencing, for instance, was in bad need of repair. Many of the posts were rotted and practically crumbling, and in some spots, the barbed wire was slack and drooping clear to the ground.

But the solitude was fantastic, the space mind-boggling. There were no traffic noises, no drunks or barroom brawls, no bank robberies or convenience store stickups, no violence or anger or people strung out on drugs.

Chase's mouth thinned. Maybe his ten years as a cop were getting to him. He specialized in narcotics because he hated drugs, users and pushers with an overwhelming passion. The newest thing on the street was called ''ice,'' and it was a killer drug, hooking a person with one pop. There was satisfaction and frustration in working narcotics. Busting a major pusher was satisfying, but there was always another one to take his place.

Jude slammed into his mind. The thought of her involved with drugs created a nearly intolerable ache in his gut. Her story of fixing up the ranch to sell could be nothing more than a damn clever cover to explain her presence. If she didn't want the place, why had she kept it until now? Apparently she had inherited it from her Uncle Simon, but Uncle Simon had been dead for three years.

Chase topped a low hill, the first of the rolling land. Riding down the other side, the buildings were no longer in sight. Ahead of him, one hill blended into another. He glanced at his watch and urged Thunder into a faster pace; he needed to check these hills before starting back.

Jude's car was loaded. There was excitement lurking within her as she drove from Naples to the ranch, and there was no denying that Chase was at the heart of the sensation.

Whether it was sensible or not, she liked him. She liked his weird sense of humor about his dog. She liked that he had laughed when the flopping hose doused her with paint, and that he'd laughed even harder when she'd doused him in return. She liked his looks. Liked? Lord above, she *loved* his looks. As for sex appeal, when had she ever felt so much from a man's smile? Or merely because he looked at her?

So he didn't have a steady job, nor seemed to have any plans to find one. Was that really a strong enough reason to disregard her feelings? True, she was putting the cart ahead of the horse. But wasn't it only natural for a thirty-year-old woman to be thinking of the future if and when she was fortunate enough to meet a man who made her very skin tingle?

With the radio playing and the car windows open, Jude arrived home. She got out humming to herself and began hauling groceries into the house.

"Chase," she yelled toward the barn after the second load. "How about giving me a hand?"

It was odd that he hadn't come out to meet her, she thought while gathering another load from the trunk of the car. The new hose for the paint sprayer was beneath the sacks of groceries. Jude made half a dozen trips to the house and finally had everything in the kitchen, including the hose.

Quickly she put the perishable items in the refrigerator and freezer, then, carrying the hose, she went to look for Chase.

Shorty, who'd been stretched out in the shade of the barn, got to his stubby legs as Jude approached, wagged his rear end and woofed. Jude managed a reasonably friendly "Hi, Shorty," but continued into the barn.

It seemed empty. "Chase?"

It *was* empty. Surprised, Jude went back outside. It was then that she saw the vacant corral. He'd gone riding? The minute her back was turned, he'd stopped working?

Disappointment welled in her throat, feeling like a huge lump. What kind of man was he that he couldn't be trusted to earn his pay without being supervised every second?

This hurt, Jude thought while clenching her fists and blinking back tears. Damn him for being an insensitive, selfish clod. Like him? She wasn't really that stupid, was she?

Disgusted with her urge to cry, Jude marched to the house. She was still putting away groceries when she looked out the kitchen window and saw Chase and Thunder returning. She froze, because even at that distance Chase's good looks battered her senses.

Shaking suddenly, Jude sat down. This was getting out of hand. She hardly knew him and nothing more romantic than one innocuous contact and a few smoldering looks had passed between them. What in God's name would happen to her self-control if he ever did more than lay his hands on her shoulders?

Chase couldn't miss Jude's car parked beside the house. In spite of some anxiety about facing her with a trumped-up story, Chase felt the satisfaction of having done his job well. He had not only located the airstrip, he'd seen indisputable proof that it had been used recently, certainly since the last rainfall.

Disturbing to realize, the last rainfall hadn't been that long ago. He would like to pinpoint a few dates: when, exactly, had it rained last, and when, exactly, had Jude come to the ranch?

He unsaddled Thunder and turned him into the corral, then put away his saddle and gave the big horse a helping of hay.

Drawing a deep breath, Chase walked to the house to get his lies to Jude over with.

Five

Jude had an air of fatalistic resignation when Chase came walking in. He was a grown man, and if this was how he behaved on the job, it was no wonder he didn't have one.

"Hi," she said coolly. With her back to him, Jude fit a box of pancake mix onto an already crammed shelf. "Did you take Thunder out for some exercise?"

Chase cleared his throat. "Uh, yeah. He has to...get some exercise every so often. Hope you don't mind."

"Were you gone long?"

"A couple of hours. Go ahead and dock today's pay, Jude. It's only fair."

"Dock your pay?" She turned to face him and felt her anger draining away at the sight of his tousled hair and long, lean body. "That's not...necessary."

"I'd feel better about it," Chase insisted.

"Isn't money important to you, Chase?" she asked softly.

Chase didn't want to start talking about money and be reminded again that she was expecting a windfall. "Sure it's important. It's pretty tough to live without money."

"But you do it," Jude said quietly. "Don't you? Most of the time? Chase, the condition of your pickup and trailer..." She stopped and turned back to the grocery-laden counter. "Forget it. How you live is none of my business."

He looked at her straight back and long, shiny hair, at her curved hips in snug jeans, and experienced an almost painful influx of desire. Why did she reach him so profoundly when other women did not? Oh, there were women in his life. He was healthy and had a normal sex drive. But he'd rarely been attracted to a woman under his investigation and certainly not to this degree.

There was another discomforting aspect to this charade developing, also. His persona of a carefree, rootless cowboy had Jude concerned. She didn't seem like a person who tried to organize other people's lives, but his devil-may-care attitude was bothering her.

"I'll get back to work now," he said quietly, wishing it weren't necessary to play this sort of game with her. Especially if she was truly unaware of the misuse of that old landing strip. "Jude...I'm sorry."

"I...don't know how to take you, Chase," she said in a near whisper.

He wanted her to turn around, but he knew better than to physically urge her to do so. "Look at me, Jude," he requested softly.

She turned slowly.

"When did you come here?" he asked.

Her lips parted in surprise. "I beg your pardon?"

"When, exactly, did you come to the ranch?" Chase repeated.

What a strange question. Perplexed and wounded that he would come up with something so impersonal after her remark about not knowing how to take him, Jude returned her attention to the groceries on the counter. "What difference does that make?" Her voice wasn't altogether kind and her hands fluttered uselessly. She looked at him again. "Why do you want to know?"

"I'm only curious. Is there some reason you'd rather not talk about it?"

"For Pete's sake," Jude exclaimed. "Do you always talk in riddles?" Her voice became impatient. "I don't remember what day I got here. Do you want me to figure it out for you?"

Chase did want her to figure it out, but pushing too hard for information would only arouse her suspicions. Maybe he'd already done that, he thought while watching the spark of resentment in her eyes. He didn't like questioning her, or suspecting her, and he tried to cover the turmoil in his own system by mumbling, "It doesn't really matter. I was only trying to calculate work versus time."

"Calculate what?" Jude asked sharply.

"Uh, how much work you've accomplished in comparison to the amount of time you've been here."

That was a barefaced lie, Jude realized with a sinking sensation. He was speaking gibberish, lying to beat the band, and why? What possible benefit could he receive from such an inane lie? Did it have something to do with why he took time off today, and where he might have gone?

She didn't know or understand him, and yet she couldn't look at him without wanting him. The term *wanting him* beat in her brain, repeating itself like an echo and rocking her very foundation. Her lips felt dry, and she wet them with the tip of her tongue while her heartbeat pounded in her own ears. She had never just *wanted* a man before. Her relationships had been rather ordinary, certainly without the raging fever scorching her now.

It embarrassed her. What if he could tell what she was thinking? "Please," she said huskily. "Go...do something. Lunch will be ready in about twenty minutes. I—I'll ring the gong.''

Chase's hands were at his sides, and they suddenly ached with the need to touch her. ''Jude...'' He took a step forward.

She watched him, intently, but didn't move out of his way. She couldn't. ''Chase...''

''Jude...''

''Chase...''

They sounded, she thought numbly, like a broken record. The same emotions she had been struggling with were on his face, in his eyes, in the reluctant line of his lips.

And then, as though someone or something had pushed a button marked Go, they rushed forward and into each other's arms. It wasn't a simple embrace. Their arms got tangled, and neither seemed able to find the other's mouth. Kisses fell on chins and cheeks and noses. Their thighs bumped. Chase felt an elbow in his ribs. Jude's breasts seemed utterly flattened by something heavy.

But neither could back off from the other and, finally, their lips met. Jude's knees grew weak. Chase's tongue pushed into her mouth, and she curled one foot up around his leg and leaned into him. Moaning hoarsely, she moved against him, igniting flames in her own breasts by rubbing them against his chest.

Chase was seeing stars. He'd expected fireworks, but nothing like this. His head was spinning like a top, and he marveled that the seams of his jeans held the power of his arousal.

His hands skimmed down her back to her hips and hauled her closer... closer. She snuggled and moved and emitted husky little moans that had him gasping for air.

''Jude... baby.''

''Oh, Chase, Chase.''

They stopped attempting speech and kissed again, wildly, with tongues and lips and bodies. Chase yanked the bottom of her blouse from the waistband of her jeans and felt his shirt being dislodged in the same hasty way. He found bare skin beneath the blouse, hot, silky skin that nearly tore off the top of his head. Jude wanted to rip the clothes from his body and did her utmost to do so. They were gasping and panting and groping and kissing, all at the same time.

Jude broke away first and grabbed his hand, whispering breathlessly, "My room is upstairs."

Dazed, Chase let her lead him from the kitchen. He needed all of her so badly he hurt. He needed her naked and lying beneath him. He needed . . .

He stopped at the foot of the stairs. Jude tugged on his hand. "Chase?"

"Wait . . . wait a minute, honey."

"Wait? For what?" Jude smiled dreamily and brought his hand up to her chest, nestling it between her breasts.

He nearly choked. Her heat seemed to engulf him, and her scent was fogging his brain.

But his internal battle continued. He spoke automatically, raggedly, and heard the words coming out of his mouth as though someone else was saying them. "I . . . can't. My back. Doctor's orders."

Jude stared. "Your doctor ordered you to avoid making love?"

"Adamantly." Choice swallowed and tried to grin. "Uh, feels kind of awkward, doesn't it?"

Dropping his hand, Jude brought hers to her throat. Her fingertips absentmindedly caressed the dampness of her own skin while she tried to calm her racing pulse. "Why . . . why did you kiss me?"

"I didn't think." That much, at least, was true. For some reason he had stopped thinking. He would pay a price for this episode. A cold shower wasn't going to cool him off, not *ten* cold showers.

But if ever a man deserved the agony of unfulfilled passion, it was him.

"I'd better get out of here," he said with a look that pleaded for understanding, which was phony through and through. If Jude ever really understood him, she'd probably kick his butt clear into the next county.

Nervously she twisted a lock of her hair. Her nod was barely perceptible and without confidence.

Spinning on his heel, Chase returned to the kitchen and hit the screen door almost running. Outside, Shorty yapped a cheerful greeting, but Chase didn't slow down till he reached the bunkhouse, where he went in and slammed the door behind him.

Jude continued up the stairs, moving like a sleepwalker. She went into the bathroom and splashed cool water on her feverish face, then stared at herself in the mirror. Her confusion was glaringly obvious.

She put her face in her hands and groaned. That had been crazy downstairs, unbelievable. No man had ever brought out that side of her before. Had it been lurking in her system all along, lying in wait for the right spark?

Chase was the right spark, but maybe he didn't want to be. Had his doctor really ordered him to abstain from sexual activity? Why was she having so much trouble believing him? Surely he wouldn't inflict this sort of embarrassment and physical anguish upon either of them without good cause.

Jude sighed as her thinking swayed in Chase's favor. Poor guy. His back must have been seriously injured in that fall. He never appeared to be in pain, but some people were so courageous, and so private, that others never knew how they suffered. Apparently he could still ride a horse, although a normal ride was a far cry from hanging on to the back of a bucking bronco.

He was probably terribly embarrassed right now. She would do her best to put him at ease during lunch, Jude generously decided.

And her next sigh contained a bit of pathos, because it was unquestionably best for her that Chase's bad back had stopped him at the foot of the stairs.

When Chase heard the gong announcing lunch about a half hour later, he fought a tide of distaste at facing Jude so soon. His nerves were raw and on edge, and he couldn't curse his abysmal lack of control enough.

But he was making headway in his investigation, and if that snitch's story was true to the end, another shipment of heroin would be coming in very soon. He had to smooth things over with Jude. By now she had to be feeling some resentment. It was only natural that she blame him for the embarrassment of being turned down, however imaginative his lies had been to keep from going up those stairs with her.

What should his mood be when he walked into her kitchen again? Lighthearted? Or heavy because his activities were so painfully restricted by an emotionless doctor?

Maybe cocky. Joking. Grinning.

Chase muttered a vile word. He felt as much like grinning right now as he did when he busted a kingpin drug pusher, without any of the satisfaction. There was nothing remotely amusing in the present situation. He wanted a woman he didn't dare touch. If he had gone up those stairs and made love to Jude Colter, the case he was building against whoever was smuggling drugs onto her land could be in the trash bin. Especially if she was involved.

His system rebelled whenever he put Jude in that scenario, but he didn't dare overlook any possibility at this stage of his investigation. And one thing he'd learned through years of police work, anything *was* possible.

How he managed to look innocent, Chase would never know. But he walked into Jude's kitchen sniffing the air. "Smells good in here."

"Corned beef," Jude explained. "The Naples market has a pretty decent deli, and I bought some corned beef and potato salad for lunch. Sit down and make a sandwich. There's rye bread, too." She noted that Chase's eyes didn't quite connect with hers, and her heart nearly melted with compassion for his discomfort.

They sat at the table. Jude put on a purposely bright expression. "Please don't be embarrassed about what happened," she said while shaking out her napkin. "I understand, perfectly."

Chase did a double take. He'd thought *she* would be the embarrassed one. The resentful one. There was no sign of either emotion on her beautiful face.

He felt something crumpling within him. Jude Colter had the power to undermine every one of his personal rules and regulations. If she wasn't a suspect in a very serious investigation, he would leap over this table in a single bound and make love to her until they were both exhausted.

Only, desire for her sexy body wasn't the only thing he was feeling for Jude. Chase uneasily recognized tenderness when looking at her, an urge to protect her, another to help her with her goal for the ranch, yet another to share lovers' confidences with her.

In short, he was getting in damned deep. How in hell had this sticky situation developed so fast?

Jude passed the plate of corned beef. "Eat . . . and enjoy."

Chase accepted the plate. "Thanks."

That afternoon Jude decided to scrape loose paint from the exterior of the toolshed while Chase hammered loose boards in the barn's rickety structure. She could hear him working and tried not to dwell on the thought that the barn would've probably been ready for painting if he hadn't taken a horseback ride instead of doing his job this morning.

Biscuit appeared and rubbed against Jude's ankles while she wielded the paint scraper. Since Shorty's arrival, Biscuit was rarely seen, which was upsetting to Jude. Her cat had always followed her around like a second shadow, and now the poor thing was afraid to come out of the barn. Shorty was a scamp, and if he had any intelligence whatsoever, Jude couldn't see it.

But Chase loved his dog, just as she loved Biscuit. His truck and trailer might be on the verge of sudden death, but he took very good care of his animals.

Jude turned to look at the handsome horse in the corral and instead spotted Shorty hightailing it across the compound as fast as his stubby legs could carry him. "Biscuit!" Jude shrieked, because the big cat seemed unaware of Shorty's fierce charge. Dropping the paint scraper, Jude tried to scoop up Biscuit, but the cat neatly sidestepped the attempt and poised herself to give battle.

The pudgy pooch came to a screeching halt about five feet away. His rear end was wagging all over the place, and to Jude's astonishment, he seemed to be grinning. Biscuit was on the very tips of her toes with her back arched. Her right front paw came up with claws unfurled as she hissed a challenge at Shorty.

"Well, for heaven's sake," Jude said under her breath, and then laughed. "Guess you can take care of yourself just fine, eh, Biscuit?" She sent Shorty a smug look. "And you, my friend, don't scare..."

Just then Shorty took off, and so did Biscuit. Only now the cat was chasing the dog.

Jude started laughing and couldn't stop. The two animals went around and around a pole in the compound, first one way and then the other, with Shorty doing the chasing for a while and then Biscuit.

The barking and laughter brought Chase out of the barn. "What's going on out here?" He saw Jude leaning against the toolshed, nearly doubled over with laughter. She spotted him and pointed. Chase started laughing, too.

But he just wasn't as receptive to a hearty laugh as Jude was, no matter how cute Shorty and Biscuit were, and after a minute he went into the barn and whacked the hell out of a loose board with his hammer.

The following morning, bright and early, Chase started the paint sprayer. Before the sun went down that evening, the barn was painted. The next day he did the toolshed, the larger shed containing the tractor, and the bunkhouse.

Jude was utterly amazed. In two days every building had a fresh coat of paint, other than the house. At this astonishing rate, her renovations would be completed in less than a week. And...there would no longer be a reason for Chase to hang around.

The thought was shattering. In less than a week Chase Sutton would lead Thunder into his horse trailer, take his gear and his dog, climb into his old pickup and drive away.

Jude's soul rebelled. It was too soon. She wasn't ready for Chase to leave. She never should have allowed him to monkey around with that old paint sprayer. Without it, the two of them would have painted buildings for weeks yet.

In a very short time she had grown accustomed to Chase's presence. And Shorty's. Even Biscuit didn't mind having a dog on the place anymore, even though their interaction never went beyond chasing each other until they were both limp with exhaustion.

On Saturday night Jude told Chase to sleep in the next morning. They were outside, standing near the back door of the house. Darkness was encroaching. Supper was over and Chase had given Shorty the bone from the beef roast Jude had prepared.

"Sleep in?" Chase echoed. "I thought we'd probably get started on the house tomorrow."

"Tomorrow is Sunday, Chase."

"Well, yes, but..." He cleared his throat. "I'll do whatever you say." It had suddenly occurred to him that a whole day would be time enough to scrupulously check the area around the landing strip, which he'd been thinking might be well worth the effort.

"The house is going to take a lot more work than the other buildings, Chase. All of the windows have to be masked off, and unless we paint the trim white along with the siding, we'll have to paint around it."

"Once it's masked, the sprayer will make quick work of the siding, Jude. The trim will take the most time."

Their conversation seemed to be on a whole other level than what they were both thinking. For certain, painting the house wasn't what was on Jude's mind, and from the sexually charged vibes she was picking up from Chase, painting wasn't his uppermost thought, either.

It was this way every single time they stopped working long enough to talk about anything... every time they sat down to the table together... each and every time they happened to touch. Always accidentally, of course. Not once since that wild kissing session in the kitchen had either of them deliberately touched the other.

Jude couldn't stop herself from making herself very feminine for the evening meal. She always showered, fixed her hair, and wore makeup and a dress. Wondering if she wasn't purposely trying to tempt Chase into forgetting his doctor's orders, and even feeling a little guilty about it, she couldn't seem to halt the practice.

Tonight her dress was a simple blue shirtwaist with a full skirt, but the bodice shaped to her breasts in a beguiling manner, of which Jude was completely aware. Their gazes, both Chase's and Jude's, were on Shorty and his beef bone, which had instantly become beloved property to the little pooch.

"I was thinking," Jude murmured. "Maybe we could take a drive tomorrow."

Chase's eyes jerked from Shorty to Jude. "A drive?"

Bravely, Jude faced him. "There's a ghost town not too far away. We could visit it."

Chase looked away. "I've seen all the ghost towns in Nevada, Jude." Wishing he could spend the day with her, without the concerns he'd brought here with him, only gave him a knot in his gut. If he wasn't going to paint tomorrow, he had to do some more snooping.

"Oh." His refusal hurt and needed no analysis. He didn't want to spend his free time with her and that was that. "Well...maybe you would rather work and get this job over with," she said huskily.

"No, I'd really like to take Thunder out for a long ride," Chase replied through clenched teeth without looking at her. And then, because he knew her feelings were hurt, he added, "Too bad we don't have another horse. You could go with me."

Jude's eyes widened. "Do you mean that? You really wouldn't mind if I went along?"

A warning buzzer went off in Chase's head. He'd obviously spoken too hastily. "Um . . . sure. But you don't have a horse."

"But I can get one. Chase, about ten miles down the road is a ranch that rents out horses. We could go right now and bring one back in your trailer. Then we'd be all ready for morning. Oh, this is great! Wait here, and I'll run and get some money."

"Aw, hell," Chase muttered as Jude dashed into the house on flying feet. How was he going to look around that landing strip with Jude in tow?

Unless . . . ? Frowning speculatively, Chase let his mind take him beyond his initial glimmer of an idea. Having Jude along might be the smartest thing he could do at this point. She was bound to react when they "stumbled" across the landing strip. Maybe she would even attempt to keep him from seeing it. He could pick up countless clues about what was going on merely by watching Jude tomorrow.

He could if he stayed alert to more than her femininity, Chase thought wryly. Ignoring her scent and the heat that seemed to shimmer from her exciting body was getting harder to do. It wasn't so bad when he was working. For hours on end during the past few days he had held that sprayer nozzle like a weapon, losing himself in the numbing process of watching red paint flow over old boards.

But he had come to both dread and yearn for the evening meal, when she turned domestic and sinfully sexy at the same time. How could a plain blue dress, which she was wearing tonight, make him think of wild, raw sex? How many times recently had he nearly lost control because she moved her head just so and her soft, sensuous hair caressed her cheek?

With a grim expression, Chase left the back of the house to hitch the horse trailer to his pickup. One thing was certain: he wasn't going to easily walk away from the Colter Ranch and forget Jude. And it just might be the most sorrowful day of his life if he learned, for certain, that drugs were being dropped on her land with her knowledge.

Jude came out, saw what Chase was doing, and felt her interior ooze together in a rush of pure pleasure. He *did* want her to go with him tomorrow. It was going to be a fabulous day, and she wasn't going to worry about his lackadaisical life-style or how quickly his departure date was creeping up, either.

After all, they were only going to be riding horses together. Who could possibly find anything emotionally threatening in a horseback ride?

Six

Jude was up early the next morning. She happily hummed to herself while preparing a big lunch to take on the ride. The rented horse was in the corral with Thunder, and while it was obvious that Thunder was king of the hill out there, he tolerated the newcomer as long as he didn't intrude on Thunder's space.

With lunch packed and the coffee brewing, Jude dashed upstairs to finish getting ready for the day. Already she was wearing old jeans and boots, but she had decided to take care of her and Chase's lunch before doing her face and hair.

Of course, she had no intention of slathering her face with makeup, but highlighting her features with subtle touches of cosmetics was only normal for a date.

That's what today felt like, an honest-to-gosh date. Jude couldn't deny the excitement in her system. The Chase she was getting to know and like so much seemed strangely disconnected from his careless past. Look how hard, how steadily, he had worked during the past few days. Look how much he had accomplished. The man had untapped talents, obviously, and hordes of determination with the right incentive.

Jude frowned over the word *incentive*. It had popped into her mind rather automatically, but once there, didn't feel quite right. What possible incentive could be influencing Chase to work hard out here? Not twenty bucks a day and her cooking, that was certain.

Could it be . . . her? Dare she even think that Chase was finding something on the Colter Ranch that had totally bypassed him until he had met her?

Or was she only wishing that were the case?

A few minutes in front of the bathroom mirror with her assortment of cosmetics improved Jude's exterior, but a little of her previous excitement had faded in the process. She mustn't expect more from Chase than he was willing to give, she told herself. A leopard didn't easily change his spots, and Chase just might be the sort of cat who preferred a solitary, totally unattached life, however affectionate he became with a woman.

Downstairs again, Jude started breakfast. When Chase came walking in, the bacon was ready and she was ladling pancake batter onto the griddle.

"Good morning," she sang out brightly.

"Morning."

"Sit down. I'll get you some coffee."

"I can get it." Chase took his mug from the table and brought it to the coffeepot on the counter. He was thrilled to see pancakes instead of oatmeal, although he'd eaten Jude's oatmeal the past two mornings and had to admit the gunky stuff was more tolerable with brown sugar.

Jude kept sending him admiring glances. He looked as crisp as cracked ice this morning, clean-shaven, lean and lanky in worn jeans and a white Western-cut shirt. In his presence, she realized with a blossoming of renewed excitement, she felt pretty, and appealing in a completely female way.

"Need any help?" Chase asked while taking a cautious but life-giving swallow of his hot coffee.

"Everything's under control. Go ahead and sit down. This batch of cakes will be done in a jiffy."

He obeyed by taking his place at the table. But the sweet little swishing of Jude's behind as she tended to the pancakes seemed to be the only thing in the kitchen to look at, and he grumpily brought the mug of coffee to his lips for a healthy swig.

Jude, he noticed wryly, didn't seem at all grumpy this morning. It wasn't quite as early as they'd been starting the day, but it was early enough that he didn't feel like belting out a song.

It was obvious that she was looking forward to their day together, and the whole fiasco was digging a hole in Chase's gut. If Jude was ignorant of the drug trade on her land, she didn't deserve what he was doing to her. Lies, pretense and deliberate deception had never bothered him when dealing with a suspect, especially when he obtained positive results and the suspect ended up in a jail cell.

But there was something guileless about Jude, in spite of her occasionally evasive or strange remark. If she was totally innocent and falling for him, he would never forgive himself. Despising himself wouldn't make her feel any better, though.

He would watch his step today, Chase concluded. There would be no flirting, no fooling around with innuendo, no unnecessary touching, and for certain, no clinches.

Jude brought a platter of pancakes to the table with a wide, excited smile. "Let's eat. I'm anxious to get started on our ride."

The weather was perfect for an outing. They weren't very far from the compound before Chase began relaxing. He did love riding, especially in country like this where the sounds and scents came strictly from nature. A man could live out his life happy on a place like this, he thought. He glanced at Jude and silently added, *Particularly if she was here with him.*

He clenched his jaw and turned his thoughts.

Jude's spirit was so alive she felt close to bursting. Her rented horse seemed extraordinarily handsome, although labeling his gait as smooth would be a little farfetched. The animal had a roll and a bounce to his step that jolted Jude's spine, and she didn't have to ponder the matter to know how stiff and sore she was going to be by tonight.

It would be worth it, though. It had been ages since she had done anything so marvelous as riding along beneath a perfect sky with a gorgeous man. The solitude seemed to unite her and Chase in some mysterious way, drawing them emotionally closer. Did he feel it?

Smiling softly, Jude turned her head to look at him. Sensing her scrutiny, Chase said the first thing that popped into his brain. ''The fencing's in bad shape, Jude.''

''The fencing?'' Her eyes darted to the nearby line of bedraggled posts and barbed wire. ''Oh, yes, I know. But:..'' She abruptly halted the explanation on the tip of her tongue, the one about her decision to ignore the fencing because she could only go so far with renovations, as an idea had suddenly sprouted. ''It will take a lot of work to repair,'' she said instead.

Chase gave her a raised-eyebrow look. ''Are you planning to repair it?''

''Of course,'' Jude replied smoothly, as though replacing posts and barbed wire had been a part of her plans all along. The extensive job would completely deplete her bank account, but Chase wouldn't be leaving when the painting was done. Her mood, which she had thought was already as high as it could get, was suddenly on a whole other plane, one that had her soaring.

"Guess I misunderstood," Chase said. "I thought you were only going to do the buildings."

Jude sent him a dazzling smile. "You'll stay and help, won't you? I couldn't do it without you, Chase."

"Uh, probably."

His response wasn't as enthusiastic as Jude would have preferred, but it was possible, she thought, that he needed to think about it a little. After all, he was still a leopard with pretty solidly set spots.

She laughed for the pure joy of doing so. If it wouldn't look so silly, she would fling her arms wide and attempt to embrace the day. She couldn't remember the last time she'd felt so carefree and happy. If she ever had, she amended. Certainly it had never happened because of a man.

"Something funny?" Chase queried, wondering what he might have missed.

"I just felt like laughing."

Chase couldn't stop himself from looking at her. They had both put on hats for the ride. Jude's was straw and had a red scarf tied around its crown that hung down her back in two sassy tails. Her hair had been tucked up beneath the hat, although some of it had refused to stay confined and had slipped down to dance in the gentle breeze. The way her thighs curved around her horse's back was positively sinful, although how else she might sit escaped Chase. It was just that she was becoming prettier and sexier with each passing day, and if he got this case wrapped up and himself off the Colter Ranch without making love to Jude, he would put himself up for sainthood.

"What?" Jude asked at the extended inspection she was getting, though it gladdened her heart to the explosive point. She knew he wanted to kiss her, how could she not? Kissing, and much more, was in the air every time they went near each other. If it wasn't for his doctor's orders, they would have already made love.

"Nothing," Chase said almost angrily, jerking his head around to face front.

Jude smiled serenely. His anger could only be directed at his doctor, after all. There wasn't a reason in the world for him to be upset with her.

When they'd started out from the compound, Jude hadn't sensed any pattern to their ride. But she was picking up adjustments in direction, all Chase's doing, and while she really didn't care where they rode, she was curious.

"Are we going any place in particular?" she inquired, and then smiled. "Maybe to something you saw the other day when you were exercising Thunder?"

Chase sent her a sharp glance. "You must know the ranch. Where do you think we're going?"

Jude laughed and shook her head. "I know the compound, Chase. This is all new to me."

"But you lived here."

"How much do you remember of your surroundings at five years of age?" she teased.

He wanted to believe her, desperately, in fact. But she was bound to deny familiarity with the place if she didn't want anyone recognizing her knowledge of the airstrip.

"I'm not heading anywhere special," he said grouchily.

"Sounds to me like you didn't have enough coffee before we left the house," Jude observed in an amused tone.

Chase stared straight ahead.

Chuckling under her breath, Jude casually glanced behind them. "Oh, for heaven's sake," she exclaimed. "Would you look at who's following us?"

Chase turned in the saddle and then yelled, "Shorty, get yourself back to the ranch!"

The dog stopped walking, but instead of turning around, he sat down.

"He doesn't mind very well, does he?" Jude commented.

Chase pulled Thunder to a halt and frowned back at Shorty. Jude reined in her horse. "Guess he didn't want to be left behind," Chase said.

"He'll get tired if he follows us all day."

"Yeah, but I guess he can ride with me if he can't keep up. Come on, Shorty," he yelled. "You can come along."

Gleefully, Shorty bounded forward. Jude shook her head as the ugly little mutt ran up grinning. "He's got you snowed," she told Chase.

"Nah, he's one of the good guys."

"And what," Jude questioned dryly, "do you consider to be the bad guys in the animal world?"

"No bad guys in the animal world, Jude. Not like the vultures in human society."

Jude cocked an eyebrow. "I didn't know you were a philosopher, Chase."

"Lots about me you don't know, honey."

It was the God's truth, Jude realized with a spurt of uneasiness when they were under way again. She was functioning strictly on feelings where Chase was concerned. He was good-looking and sexy, and her hormones were responding. Their relationship was so basic as to be laughable. He was male, she was female, and that was about it.

Trying to recapture her previous mood, Jude sighed. She was strangely resigned to the situation. If the opportunity arose to make love with Chase, she wouldn't say no. Anything beyond that was no more than a pretty unlikely fantasy, and if she happened to fall in love with him, which she feared she was on the verge of doing, she would have to suffer the consequences, and do so all by herself because he would be gone.

They were approaching a series of softly rolling hills. "It's beautiful out here," Jude said quietly.

"Yeah, it is."

Shorty was lingering to sniff at every bush and then running to catch up. The horses plodded along. The warm breeze carried the smell of soil and growing things, and regardless of the pocket of doubt about Chase's life-style pestering Jude, it was still the most glorious day in her memory.

They stopped at a narrow little creek to give the horses a drink. Jude dismounted and felt her joints protesting the long ride.

Chase opened his canteen for a drink and then passed it to Jude. "Thirsty?"

She had her own canteen, but she took Chase's with a sensually inquisitive look into his eyes. "Thanks."

The second their eyes met, Chase thought of sex. Not just sex in general, but sex with Jude. Making love with Jude. Undressing her, undressing himself or having her do it. He thought of slow sex, and fast sex, but whatever its speed or haste, it was always hot sex. *Very* hot.

That's how it would be with her, he knew with painful conviction. Some things a man knew, some he didn't; this particular subject was as clear as crystal.

He turned away when some water from the canteen dribbled down Jude's chin and she slowly wiped it off. *He'd* like to lick it off, damn it to hell!

Jude bent down and dipped her hands into the creek water. "Oh, look, there are some baby fish swimming around."

"Minnows," Chase said sourly. "Come on, let's get going, okay?"

"Well, sure," Jude said slowly, because she couldn't think of a single reason why they should hurry today.

But she climbed back onto her horse with only one very quiet, very understated groan.

Chase heard it. "Are you all right?"

Jude shaped a big smile. "I'm perfectly all right."

"Getting stiff?"

"No. Absolutely not." Clucking to her horse, the animal fell into step a respectful distance from Thunder.

After a few minutes Shorty took off after a jackrabbit, which made Jude laugh and call, "You'll never catch him, Shorty."

They rode up the first hill and down the other side, and then another, and another. Jude eyed the trees in the distance with some longing. The sun was getting much warmer, and she wouldn't mind another break from her horse's jolting gait.

"Chase, let's ride to those trees, okay?"

Chase's gaze swung to the line of trees that followed, he knew, the configuration of the largest creek on the place.

But that creek and those trees lay in the opposite direction to the landing strip.

"Later," he said gruffly. "I want to see what's beyond these hills." If she was purposely trying to deflect his course, she wasn't going to succeed.

"Well...fine," Jude agreed reluctantly. "But then let's have lunch under those trees." Behind Jude's saddle rode a rolled blanket and the bulky sack containing lunch. She had packed plastic bags of ice among the sandwiches to keep the food cool, but as hot as the sun was becoming, the ice would last only so long.

And then they were at the crest of a sizable hill. Chase had gotten a little ahead of Jude, and she smiled, thinking that it was nice of him to stop and wait for her to catch up. She rode up next to him. "Anything interesting out here?"

Her gaze swept the area. There really wasn't anything much different beyond the hills, unless some old ruts in a flat field could be labeled interesting.

"What do you think of that?" Chase asked softly.

"Think of what, Chase?"

"Of that."

Jude frowned and took another look. "Are you talking about that field?"

She was either as innocent as a newborn or a damn fine actress, Chase thought irritably. "It's a landing strip."

"Really?" Suddenly Jude snapped her fingers. "I completely forgot. Uncle Simon was a pilot when he was a young man. I'll bet that's where he used to land his plane. But it's so far from the house, and I don't see a road, do you?"

Chase's eyes narrowed. He'd known all along that there had to be a road somewhere out here, but Jude bringing it up was startling. "Uh, yeah. Expect there is. Let's look for it."

"Look for an old road?" Jude echoed faintly. "Wouldn't you rather ride back to those trees and have lunch?"

She was tired, Chase could tell. She wasn't used to riding, and she had to be stiff and sore, even though she hadn't uttered one word of complaint.

He didn't know what to think about her complicity now. Fat lot of information he'd gotten out of watching her reaction to the landing strip. So much for his big ideas.

"What the hell?" he muttered disgustedly. "Why not? Let's go have lunch under the trees."

Jude's face brightened. "Thanks, Sutton, you're a gem!"

Yeah, a real jewel, Chase thought during the ride to the trees. Right now he'd like to forget the landing strip even existed, forget who he was and why he was out here. Cracking Jude Colter's psyche was a lost cause. To save his soul he couldn't tell whether she was the most clever criminal or the sweetest, sexiest lady he'd ever come across.

Either way he was in trouble.

This spot, Jude was convinced, was a little piece of heaven. The trees were leafed out and shading the grass in pleasantly mottled blotches of coolness. It had to be home for dozens of birds, because the twittering and cheeping was practically nonstop. The breeze rustling the leaves was like music to Jude's ears. Relaxed and drowsy, she stretched out on the blanket.

They had eaten their fill of the very good lunch she had packed, and she had put away the remnants, just in case they got hungry again before returning home. Chase had mentioned a brief walk, probably for a little privacy, Jude figured, which she herself had sought a short time ago.

Now, contented to her soul, Jude closed her eyes and listened to nature's soothing sounds—the creek, the leaves, the birds. The ordinary world seemed a million miles away. It was barely possible to even recall traffic noises or the images of a crowded shopping mall.

Jude sighed with the most peaceful sensation of her thirty years. But then, as though some part of herself wanted to disturb her serenity, her mind began to question. Would she go back to Texas when the ranch sold? If not, in which direction would she head?

It would be a different direction than Chase's. She could prolong his stay until the ranch was in shape, but then, unless something changed drastically, they would go their separate ways.

An awful ache began in Jude's chest. How far dare a woman go to let a man know she was interested? Maybe he already figured she was interested from the wild kisses they had shared in the kitchen that day, but did he have any idea how much? Did he feel anything important for her? If he did, wouldn't he find a way around his doctor's orders?

She couldn't picture Chase in a sexless love affair. If he cared for a woman, he would want to make love to her. Wasn't that what she had to discover for her own peace of mind—exactly what he did feel for her, if anything?

Chase returned and saw Jude's closed eyes. He rubbed his mouth, wondering if he shouldn't go by himself and look for that road. How long would she sleep?

But Jude's eyes didn't stay closed. They fluttered open and landed on Chase. "Hi," she said softly.

The bottom dropped out of his stomach. With one simple, everyday, two-letter word, she had proclaimed them to be the only man and woman on earth and given him the freedom to do something about it.

"Jude," he said hoarsely. "We can't..."

"I know. Your back." A hint of a smile played with her lips. "Maybe you should lie down and give your back a rest."

"Lie down?"

Jude patted the blanket beside her. "There's plenty of room."

He knew lying on that blanket was the last thing he should be doing out here, but he actually stared at the spot and considered it. His imagination leapt far ahead of his will and devised erotic images of the two of them lying together. The shape of her legs in snug denim was tantalizing. Without the denim...?

He swallowed. "Jude...I'm going to take a ride and look for that road."

She sat up. "Why?"

"Uh, just curious."

"I'm curious, too, Chase," she said in a near whisper. "Curious about you."

She couldn't have said what she wanted any plainer. Chase's pulse went crazy. His eyes darted wildly from her to a tree to another tree to the creek. How could any man refuse such an invitation? He might think about sainthood on occasion, but he knew he'd never make the grade. Not when a pair of soft brown eyes could turn his knees to water and another part of his anatomy to solid steel.

He glanced down to the front of his jeans and then at her, sitting on that blanket, all flushed and female. "Do you know what you're doing?"

Jude moistened her lips, slowly, with the tip of her tongue, which raised Chase's blood pressure another degree. "I...think so." She was beginning to wonder, though. She had never been so bold with a man, and it was all over his face that he wasn't pleased by his own physical weakness for her.

"Chase," she said in a low voice. "Is there . . . someone else? Another woman?"

"No," he finally said. "There's no one important." In the next instant he knew he should have lied. It was either get on his horse and get the hell away from Jude or become totally lost in what was making the very air around them vibrate.

His brain said *Go,* and his body was screeching *Stay!*

And then he blinked, because Jude was unbuttoning her blouse. "What're you doing?"

"That creek isn't deep enough for swimming, but it's just about right for getting wet." She smiled. "And for cooling off. Do you need to cool off, Chase? I do."

"I'm not going to cool off much if you undress," he growled.

"No?" Jude sent him another smile. "Let's find out, shall we?"

"Damn it, Jude . . ."

Never in her life had Jude deliberately teased a man by taking off her clothes. But then, never before had she been so mesmerized by a man, either. So tempted. The bulge in his jeans was fascinating, drawing her gaze again and again. He knew where she was looking, too, but Chase seemed to be as caught up in this game as she was.

The trouble was, this wasn't a game to Jude. There was something powerful between her and Chase Sutton, and she would never rest again in her entire life if she let him take Shorty and Thunder and drive off in the near future without finding out what it meant.

Today and this place were precisely the time and location to do so.

Seven

Jude stripped down to her bra and panties. Chase leaned against the trunk of a nearby tree and watched, but he never made a move toward her. It was one of those bittersweet moments that were both pleasurable and painful for a man. Particularly when the lady was so honest and had no objections to taking this to its logical conclusion.

But it was hard for Chase to break longtime rules. Not just break them, but smash them to smithereens. All of the rational arguments occurred to him while Jude was removing her clothes. Who would ever know if they made love? Not every cop was so high-minded as to keep his hands off sexy suspects. Jude was doing the inviting, and if she got hurt in the long haul, she'd have no one to blame but herself.

The argument badgering Chase the most, though, was the racking desire in his own body. He tried not to look at Jude in her lacy underwear, but he'd never seen anyone more beautiful. Her breasts were full and ripe, barely contained by a scrap of white lace, and the dark triangle between her legs was almost as obvious as the nose on her face. Her underwear was a laugh, if a painful one, and he couldn't believe she wore that sort of sexy lingerie on a daily basis.

She turned to the creek, giving him a view of her behind, which was just as arousing as her front. Then she glanced seductively over her shoulder. "Are you sure you won't change your mind about getting wet with me?"

"You're not playing fair, Jude."

"You want to, don't you?"

"Yes, I want to. I want a hell of a lot more than getting wet with you, and you know it."

"But your doctor wouldn't approve."

"That gripes the hell out of you, doesn't it?"

She shrugged, wishing she had the nerve to say, *If a couple wants to make love, they'll find a way, bad back or no bad back.* Instead she murmured, "He's your doctor." She dipped a toe into the cold creek water. "Believe me, this would cool the hottest flame."

Chase swallowed. Did he really want her *that* cooled off? Wasn't he more excited than at any time he could remember? Wasn't this just about the sexiest situation he'd ever been in?

But a douse of ice water wasn't the answer; not for him, it wasn't.

And it wasn't the answer for Jude, either.

He moved away from the tree and came up behind her. His hands slid around her waist, and he heard her swift intake of air. His head lowered to bury his face in the long, tumbled hair at the side of her throat, and he inhaled, drawing her scent deep into his lungs.

Thrilled beyond measure, Jude attempted to turn around. But he held her in place with a whispered "Wait," and brought his hands up to cup her breasts, one around each. Instantly he felt her nipples pucker against his palms. "Be sure, Jude," he whispered. "Be sure, because I can't promise you anything."

Speech escaped her. She could repudiate what he'd said, or argue against it. Maybe laugh, as though she couldn't possibly believe he was serious. Or weep because she knew he was.

But nothing came out of her mouth beyond a small, ragged moan that seemed to have its roots in her soul. His touch; being next to him like this made everything else seem meaningless. Even his comment about promises. Did she have to have promises? She was asking for nothing right now, except for his nearness, his maleness.

He kissed her bare shoulder and then her arm as she brought it up to twine around his neck. "Jude? Did you understand what I said?"

Her eyes were closed. She was leaning back against him. Without question, he was keeping her on her feet, curving his own body around hers to give her support.

His embrace wasn't completely altruistic, however. Curling his lap around Jude's bottom was like connecting two live wires. Chase wouldn't have been surprised to hear a sizzle, because he was sure feeling one.

"Must we talk?" Jude whispered.

"Not if you don't want to, baby. But tell me you heard what I said."

"I...heard."

It was all the green light Chase needed. Closing his eyes with a groan of pure pleasure, he slowly skimmed his right hand down her stomach and into her panties. "Tell me what you like," he whispered when he had found precisely what he liked.

"I like that," she gasped as he began a slow, sure stroking. "Chase...I can't stand here with you doing that."

He turned her around, quickly, almost roughly, and caught her in his arms when the impetus propelled her forward. His mouth covered hers at once. Jude's hands went up around his neck; as much as she needed to get closer to him, she also needed something to hang on to.

There was no hesitation in his kisses, none in hers. His tongue challenged hers while it greedily explored her mouth. Breathlessly she met his challenges and issued her own. She vaguely registered a clever hand unhooking her bra, and then Chase moving her slightly so the garment would fall away.

She was naked to the waist and it wasn't fair that he was fully clothed. There was no time between kisses for words, but none were needed. Jude managed to stay upright and unbutton his shirt, no small feat when her legs felt like soft rubber.

Her lips left his to bestow feverish kisses on his bare chest. She fumbled with the buckle on his belt, and shuddered when he twisted enough to wet the crest of her breast with his tongue.

He bent over then, placed an arm behind her knees and lifted her up and off the ground. Her eyes widened. "Your back!"

He laughed deep in his throat and carried her to the blanket, where he set her on her feet. When he let go of her, she sank to the blanket and watched him shed his shirt and toss it to the ground. His boots went next, yanked off impatiently, his socks, as well.

Without looking at her, he opened his belt buckle and then his fly. But then, while he pushed his jeans and briefs down in one motion, his eyes searched for contact with hers.

But she wasn't looking at his face, not even close. He stood there, over her, and watched her wide-eyed admiration of his body. It was the same way he looked at her, he realized, with awe and desire and emotions he wasn't quite sure how to categorize. Lust, yes. Without question they had something special in the chemistry department.

And maybe he'd better leave it at that, he thought, bringing himself down to the lush and eager woman on the blanket. Jude lay back, opening her arms to him. He ignored the expanse of empty blanket on either side of her and nestled himself on top of her. Hungrily he took her mouth in a long and passionate kiss. At the same time, he wriggled her panties down her hips, and what happened to them after that he didn't worry about.

Jude kicked them away without a qualm. Her heart was pounding so hard she could hear it in her own ears. She couldn't lie still, not when her bare skin was connected to so many marvelous points of nude masculinity.

She had to be in love with Chase, she thought ardently. She couldn't feel this much for a man without love. She couldn't want him until she ached, nor lie in the open with him stark naked, nor wish that it could last forever, not if she didn't love him, she couldn't.

He drove her mad by sucking on her breasts, by sucking on her tongue, by kissing her senseless, and then doing it all again. And his hands were everywhere, igniting flames wherever they lingered.

It was Jude who finally gasped, "Chase . . . do it. I'm on fire."

He groped for his jeans and dug for his wallet. Jude's eyes were so filled with passion, she barely registered him taking care of protection. Later she would thank him, she thought dizzily. But now she didn't care about anything but the desperate need tearing her apart.

She moaned at his penetration, and then wrapped her arms around him in an almost choking embrace. This was not ordinary lovemaking to Chase. He was stunned by the intensity of emotion in both himself and Jude. Hers was evident from the low, throaty sounds she was making. His had him worried about going over the edge too soon, before he gave her satisfaction. He worried about a few other things, too, like the hard ground she was lying on, and how she was going to feel after this was over.

But the pleasure was stronger than the worry, and in minutes there was nothing in his mind *but* pleasure. Nothing but the rippling heat, and the need for more...and more of the woman beneath him.

Jude climbed to the pinnacle faster than she thought possible. The world exploded within her own body, down low, and then spiraled outward and upward in rapturous waves. Chase took her cries with an openmouthed kiss, and then had to break the bond for his own explosion.

The delicious spasms slowed gradually for Jude, and were still occurring long after Chase lay on top of her, exhausted and still. She felt tears of wonder seeping from her closed eyes and didn't possess the strength to brush them away.

Her eyes fluttered open after a while, and she gazed up at the pattern of leaves and blue sky overhead. She felt deliciously loose and mellow, and she wanted to share this special moment with Chase.

"Chase?" she said softly.

He lifted his head, took one look at her ecstatic face and groaned, "Aw, hell. What've I done?"

Startled to her soul, Jude's expression lost all sense of the joy she'd been feeling. "What...what's wrong?"

She received no answer. Chase deserted her in one fluid movement, grabbed his clothes and walked into the trees. Jude lay there, so stunned she could barely breathe. He was questioning what he had done, but why?

Her mind raced for an answer that made some sort of sense. Maybe he wasn't as unattached as he'd said. Maybe there *was* someone else, a lover, a wife? Jude felt a rush of tears, but the perturbing picture of herself lying there naked and weeping pushed her to her feet. Quickly she grabbed her clothes and yanked them on.

She was sitting on the blanket to pull on her boots when Chase appeared. He bent over and snagged his hat from the ground.

Jude stood. "You could at least have the decency to look at me."

Chase's lips were in a thin, hard line. "This shouldn't have happened."

"Would you mind telling me why?" Jude's voice cracked. "Are you married?"

"God, no! I already told you that. Jude, all I can do is apologize."

Her eyes began blazing. "Oh, don't apologize for something that *I* caused. You tried to avoid it. I'm the fool here, Chase, not you."

"That's where you're wrong," he said bitterly, and slapped his hat onto his head. "I'm not ready to go back to the ranch. What do you want to do?"

Obviously this was the end of their perfect day. Jude bent over to grab the blanket, which she gave an angry shake. "Don't worry about me," she said coldly. "I can find my own way home just fine."

Chase muttered a curse under his breath. He was furious at himself, not at her, but the symptoms were close enough that Jude couldn't tell the difference. She was hurting, and he felt like a horse's hind end. Yes, she'd caused their collision, but he could have walked away before it got out of hand.

Then a new notion intruded. Maybe she'd thought occupying him with her sexy body would keep him from searching for that road. He looked away from her, despising the way his mind worked sometimes. Deep down—and maybe not so deep down—he didn't really believe Jude was implicated in the drug scheme. But he was so accustomed to turning every rock over three times before proclaiming it vermin-free, it wasn't in him to deviate from routine with a suspect.

On the other hand, he had deviated plenty, and he'd ended up hurting Jude and giving himself the start of an ulcer.

"Shorty!" he yelled, because Shorty wasn't anywhere in sight.

Jude gave him a so-now-you're-yelling-at-your-own-pet look. Her expression clearly said that he was a jerk and incapable of tender feelings.

Chase had to clamp his lips together to stop himself from telling her otherwise. It was a despicable situation, because even if Jude's innocence was proven beyond a shadow of a doubt at the conclusion of this miserable job, she would be so wounded by his deception, she would probably loathe the ground he walked on.

Shorty ran up, panting and grinning. Chase gave Jude one last look. "I'm sorry. That's all I can say right now."

Jude watched him walk to where they had left the horses. "Keep your apologies," she whispered. "Shove them up your nose." She waited until Chase had mounted and rode away before going to her own horse.

While tying the blanket behind the saddle, Jude couldn't help keeping an eye on Chase's retreat. Where was he going? Apparently he enjoyed riding around the countryside, which was understandable on such a beautiful day. But he seemed so intense about it, as though it was something he had to do.

Shorty was lagging behind Thunder, and Jude saw the little dog stop suddenly and look back at her. Chase happened to glance behind him at the same moment. "Shorty," he called.

But Shorty was undecided about which direction he preferred, and Jude felt a perverse glee that Chase's dog might choose following her instead of him. "Come on, boy," she said softly, much too quietly for Chase to hear. In the next instant Shorty bounded her way, and although Chase was too far away to see it, Jude sent him a triumphant look.

"Guess he wants to go with you," Chase yelled. "Keep an eye on him, okay?"

"I *always* keep an eye on dumb animals," Jude yelled back, and then felt petty for picking on Shorty's intelligence just because she hated his master.

In fact, she hated herself much more. She'd behaved like a slut—Jude cringed at the word—and shouldn't expect to be treated like anything else.

Mounted and riding toward home, with Shorty trotting along behind, Jude finally let the tears escape. Never had she behaved so brazenly with a man, so shamefully. She would rue this day for the rest of her life, and never would she repeat it. Never!

With so much animosity between them now, Chase would probably pack his things and leave. Jude sighed and wiped her eyes. As angry and hurt as she was, the thought of never seeing Chase again stung. She had to question her own good sense, but the truth was, she cared about him. How could she? How could she both hate and love someone?

He must never know. She had *some* pride, after all, although anyone would have been hard-pressed to locate it about an hour ago, when she was teasing and taunting Chase into making love to her.

God, she would never get over this. Whether Chase stayed or left, she would never, ever heal from this fiasco.

Canine whimpers drew Jude out of her self-pitying reverie. She stopped her horse and glanced back to see Shorty lying on his belly with his face on his paws, looking positively pathetic.

"You're tired, aren't you?" Jude accused. Shorty raised his head and cocked it to one side. "And I suppose you want to ride now," Jude went on. After a minute, with a heavy sigh, Jude slid to the ground. "Come on, let's see if I can lift a tub of lard and climb back on a horse at the same time."

As stiff and sore as she had feared that morning, Jude lay in a hot bath. Her aches weren't all from riding a horse with a bumpy gait, though. Making love on the ground had had something to do with her discomfort.

But even with aching muscles and an enormous regret eating her up, Jude couldn't help getting goose bumps when she thought of Chase's lovemaking. By her own response and pleasure, he was an incredible lover. If this one day was all there ever was between them, she had, at least, experienced what most women only dreamed of—the ultimate male.

Still, it seemed so callous to place what she had felt today in Chase Sutton's arms under the Ten Most Wanted Experiences. She was not a sensualist, and she wasn't hoping to be one. Ordinarily her feet were firmly on the ground. With Chase she had strayed far afield of her normal role with men, and it wasn't sensible, either, not when she had recognized his rootless nature right from the outset.

She'd made a fool of herself today, and it hurt worse than anything she'd ever felt. It would not happen again, not with any man, but particularly not with Chase.

The rented horse had been put in the corral, and if Jude had known how to hitch Chase's trailer to his pickup, she would have hauled the animal back to its owner. If Chase should return and announce immediate plans to leave her employ, she would have to swallow her pride and ask him to first return the horse.

It galled Jude to have to ask him for anything now. She honestly didn't know how she would deal with him, should he stay. She was distressingly torn, she realized, with one part of her praying he would stay and another thinking she should tell him to get the hell off her land if he had the nerve to try it.

Haunted by her own ambivalence, Jude finally got out of the tub, dried off and got dressed. She made supper at the usual time, relying on the simple task of heating several leftover dishes, and then sat there and ate—or picked at the food—all by herself.

With no sign of Chase, she stopped pretending interest in food and got up to clear the table and do the dishes. Biscuit was given a can of tuna for her supper, and without thinking about it, Jude scraped everything from the table into a big bowl and brought it outside for Shorty.

The little dog just sat there. "Eat," Jude commanded brusquely. But Shorty, who had to be hungry, merely gave her a doleful look. "Look," Jude said, irritated. "I rode with you on my lap for miles this afternoon. Your fat little bottom didn't help my aching thighs none, Shorty Sutton, so eat your supper like a good boy and stop giving me a hard time, okay?"

Shorty leapt up as though something had just jabbed him in the rear. Jude jumped back. "Well, good grief, if you aren't the most weird animal . . ."

Then she caught on. "Ah, I see how your loving master conned me that first night. You've been trained to ignore food until someone says 'okay.'" Shorty looked up at her and grinned, and Jude's heart nearly melted for the ugly little mutt, something she would have sworn was impossible.

Bending over, she rubbed Shorty's mismatched ears. "You're a good old guy, Shorty. Sorry I didn't like you before. But you see, I've always liked cats best."

Sighing, Jude straightened and looked out into the twilight. Evidently Chase was making a full day of it. Maybe he was doing it deliberately. Maybe he planned to return after she went to bed, and to depart the ranch in the night.

Jude tossed her head and spoke out loud. "To hell with you, Chase Sutton. I can finish the painting, don't think I can't. Who needs you?"

It wasn't late, barely dark for that matter, but the house was silent and without lights. Chase unsaddled Thunder and turned him into the corral with hay and a helping of oats. Jude usually went to bed early, but Chase had visualized her

waiting and pacing tonight, probably because he felt so
damned guilty that a good tongue-lashing would almost be
welcome.

He had to clear the air with Jude, by hook or crook or
anything else he could come up with. He'd not only found
the road, he had followed it and discovered where it connected with a highway. So it was entirely possible for someone to drive onto Colter land through its rear entrance
without anyone at the compound being the wiser. Chase
figured that was what had been going on, but he still wasn't
so positive that he intended to open up with Jude. In the
meantime, he had to stay on the ranch, and after today she
just might be in the right frame of mind to kick him out of
her life and off of her property.

As he finished up with Thunder and then bent down to
give Shorty's ears a scratch, he wished Jude hadn't retired
so early. Aside from the fact that he needed to talk to Jude
and smooth her ruffled feathers, he was hungry. He was
pretty sure Jude locked the house at night, but his stomach
was empty enough that he decided to try the back door.

From her upstairs bedroom window, Jude watched him
walk from the corral to the house. His form was darker than
the night's darkest shadows, indistinguishable beyond out-
line, and still the sight of him gave Jude a tight, choked
feeling. He was going to knock on the door, the jerk, and
wake her up.

Well, *he* didn't know she wasn't sound asleep, she thought
defensively when the inanity of her observation seeped
through her anger.

She listened, but there was no sound of knocking. In
fact...

Jude frowned at the barely perceptible, muffled noises
from downstairs. He had come in. But how? She had locked
that door, as she did every night.

A chill went up her spine. He had picked the lock, or something, and he was in the house when he thought she was asleep.

This was very strange. If a discussion couldn't wait until morning, he could have beat on the door. Instead, he had let himself in by some nefarious method.

To do what?

Jude bravely pooh-poohed any danger to herself. Chase wasn't someone to fear, for heaven's sake.

But did she really know him? And hadn't she always sensed something mysterious lurking behind his ready grins?

The old house was so creaky, she couldn't tell exactly where Chase was, except for downstairs. And she had to find out. She couldn't just cower up here and pretend he wasn't down there.

With her heart pounding, Jude ignored her robe and slippers and tiptoed from the room. Every time a board creaked, she stopped to wince and listen, but she finally made it to the stairway without detection. Slowly, as silently as possible, clinging to the banister, she crept down the stairs. There were no lights on the first floor. Whatever Chase was doing, he was doing it in the dark.

Dry-mouthed, Jude stopped at the foot of the stairs to get her bearings. A small noise came from the kitchen, and she sidled along a wall in that direction. She was barely thinking now, certainly not beyond Chase being in the house without permission, or even, ostensibly, her knowledge.

Near the refrigerator, Chase froze. Someone was moving around the first floor. Jude would announce herself, so who else was in the house?

He went into full-alert mode, sinking into the shadows next to the refrigerator. It felt unnatural to be skulking around a dark house without his gun, but he had no choice. With his back to the wall, he inched his way to the open archway.

On the other side of the wall, Jude was doing the same, holding her breath, praying, oddly enough, that she wasn't going to see Chase stealing something. Though what might be worth stealing in the kitchen escaped her. In the whole house, for that matter. Other than the cash in her purse and the metal box in her closet, both of which were upstairs, a thief would reap very little bounty from the Colter household.

Near the frame of the archway, Jude listened intently. All noise in the kitchen had ceased. Chase hadn't gone outside, she was positive, so what was he doing?

He was on the exact other side of the same wall, standing near the frame of the arch, listening with even more intensity than Jude. He felt something moving by his feet, and he glanced down to see Biscuit. "Go on, get out of here," he mouthed, and nudged the cat with his boot. Something went wrong, because he stepped on Biscuit's tail and she let out an awful squawk. Jude came crashing around the arch; Chase made a dive at the same time, and they ran into each other with such force, Jude saw stars.

"Damn!" she cried.

"Thunderation!" Chase yelled. He had grabbed her by the shoulders in the collision. "Why in hell are you sneaking around in the dark?"

"Why am *I* sneaking around? At least I belong in here. Why are you sneaking around my house?"

"I was getting something to eat."

"In the dark?"

"I didn't want to wake you. When I heard someone moving around down here, I thought... Hell, I thought it was someone else," Chase said disgustedly.

Jude shook off his hands and felt for the light switch. But instantly she remembered her short nightgown and changed her mind. "What did you do to the lock on the door, break it? If you did, you're going to pay for a new one. I don't have money for..."

"It's not broken, but if it were, I'd gladly pay for it. Jude, stop this. I didn't think you'd care if I came in for something to eat. Can we have some light?"

"Leave it off. I—I'm not really covered."

And just like that, they were back along that creek, under those trees, in each other's arms. "Honey..." Chase said huskily.

Jude was afraid that if he touched her, she would forget how badly he had hurt her today. "Keep your distance, Chase," she warned. "I'm going back to bed. Eat what you want, but lock the door again when you leave." She started to leave, then hesitated. "How *did* you get through a locked door?"

"It's an old lock. It gave easily."

"What a comforting thought," Jude drawled. "Oh, by the way, are you planning to quit your job, or are you staying?"

"I'd like to stay, Jude. Is it all right? You've got a lot of fencing to repair, and I think we're both adult enough to overlook what happened today, don't you?"

She took a breath. "By all means. Believe me, I've already forgotten it."

Eight

Chase wondered if Shorty's howling that first night at the ranch hadn't been prompted by someone monkeying around out by the landing strip. Since, Shorty hadn't howled even one time, and despite the fairy tale Chase had laid on Jude about Shorty's sexual prowess, Chase couldn't come up with another reason for his pet's—as Jude had labeled it—"caterwauling."

He shut Shorty out of the bunkhouse that night. "Guard the place, old pal, and if you hear any peculiar noises, sound the alarm."

As tired as Chase was, he lay in bed in the bunkhouse, one arm crooked beneath his head, and stared into the dark. When this thing was over and Jude was proven innocent, he was going to...

He tried again. *When this thing's over, I'm going to Jude and telling her...*

The truth was, by the time it was over, Jude would probably declare open hunting season on any hombre who went by the name of Chase Sutton.

He thought of his alternatives. There were two. Tell Jude the truth right now, or keep on lying to her. Did he trust her through and through? Implicitly?

Chase groaned. He *wanted* to trust her, more than he'd ever wanted anything. No, that wasn't true. Today by that creek he'd experienced the ultimate "wanting." Just thinking of her in the house right now, in bed, wearing God knew what when she favored such flimsy underwear, made him want her again.

He didn't deserve this mess, he thought grimly. His job was important and he'd always given it his best. His own scruples were kicking him in the teeth with Jude.

But he couldn't just cast them aside, not even for her.

At last Chase fell asleep. While in the house, Jude finally fell into a troubled slumber. Curled up on the foot of Jude's bed, Biscuit slept.

And outside, proud of his position, Shorty did guard duty. But only for a while. Then, as silence prevailed in the darkness, he, too, looked for a cozy spot. Curled up in the barn, Shorty snored the night away.

Jude was all business the next morning. Privately she was relieved that Chase was staying, but she vowed he would never hear it from her lips.

She made oatmeal and set the table. Chase came in and barely said hello. She barely answered, and they sat down to a breakfast that wasn't any more silent than any other they'd shared. At least they were single-minded on morning protocol.

They drank hot, strong coffee as though it contained their day's supply of energy, and by the time the coffeepot was empty, along with their cereal bowls, they were able to look at each other across the table without flinching.

"After I return that horse you rented, should I start working on the house?" Chase asked.

"Yes." Rising, Jude began carrying dishes to the sink. "We'll mask the windows and trim."

"With what?"

"There's a stack of old newspapers and some tape in the laundry room."

"Which is where?"

Jude nodded to her left. "Through that door."

"I'll take them outside now." Chase found the newspapers, a mountain of them. "Hey, some of these papers are ten years old."

"Uncle Simon rarely threw anything away," she called. "You should have figured that out from the clutter in the toolshed."

"True," Chase mumbled.

He went through the kitchen and out the back door, loaded down with newspapers and a roll of masking tape. Jude heaved a sigh. When she looked at Chase, she thought of yesterday, and as it already felt like a habit, she didn't count on a change anytime soon.

She was going to suffer for yesterday's escapade. If something within her ignited and came alive in Chase's presence, it was just going to have to die down again. Obviously it would get no encouragement from him, and not from her more sensible side, either.

During the drive to return the rented horse, a spontaneous idea occurred to Chase. The rancher, Sam Shelton, came out to meet him, and after a few minutes of small talk, Chase said, "Sam, the Colter Ranch doesn't have a phone. Would you mind if I used yours to make a credit card call?"

Sam was a congenial sort and brought Chase into his house. "You can use this one in the kitchen, Chase."

"Thanks." Chase quickly punched a series of numbers, which included his credit card number. While the phone rang on the other end, he took a look through the window and saw Sam outside. The house was quiet, so Chase figured it was safe to talk. "Lou? Chase Sutton. Put me through to Captain Ryder. Pronto, honey."

Almost instantly Chase heard, "Sutton? You okay?"

"I'm fine. I got an unexpected opportunity to call in. Listen, I located the landing strip and a back road connecting the ranch to an old highway. It's a matter of waiting now. If Moreno's story is accurate, that shipment should be coming in anytime now."

"What about that Colter guy you mentioned? Is he in on it?"

"Uh, I'm not sure. I doubt it, but I'm not a hundred percent positive yet."

"Where're you calling from?"

"A neighboring ranch. I gotta go, Captain. Someone's coming in."

"Be careful, Sutton," Ryder said gruffly.

"Count on it."

Chase was all smiles when Sam walked in and asked, "Get your call through all right?"

"Sure did. Thanks a lot, Sam. I appreciate it."

"No problem, Chase."

Chase made tracks back to the Colter Ranch and got right to work. All morning he and Jude masked windows, doors and trim. After lunch Chase got out the paint sprayer and tackled the siding.

It went fast. As soon as the first side of the house was sprayed, Jude tore off the masking and began painting trim. She found it disturbing that she and Chase made such a good team, but it would be a lie to deny it. As a matter of fact, Chase was an exceptionally good worker.

Thoughtfully Jude lowered her brush. What about his back? He'd lifted and carried her yesterday when he hadn't had to, and he sure hauled that big sprayer around easily enough. He never once said, "Hey, Jude, my back's acting up. I'm going to take a break." Nor had she ever witnessed him holding his back, as people sometimes did with back strain.

What, precisely, was wrong with his back? What area of it had been injured in that fall he supposedly took?

Again a sense of mystery gripped Jude. Chase was hiding something, and whatever it was had caused him to regret making love yesterday. If it wasn't another woman, which he had vehemently denied, what was it?

By quitting time, Jude was resigned to another day of work on the trim. She stood back from the house and admired the fresh paint. "Looks good, don't you think?" she said when Chase walked up.

"Looks great," he agreed. "One more day and we'll be ready to start on the fencing."

"Then there's the interior of the house to do." She sighed, slipping the scarf from her head and giving her hair a shake.

Chase stared, as though he'd never seen rich, glossy hair before, a look that Jude didn't miss. Color flared in her cheeks, and she lifted her chin in defiance of her own foolish response to a man she'd be an idiot to trust again.

"I'm going in to start supper," she announced coolly.

After a second, he nodded. "I'll be up after I shower."

"Please listen for the gong," Jude said over her shoulder as she walked away.

It was a request that neatly put him in his place, but Chase couldn't take offense. Jude would have been justified in declaring all-out war today, and she'd treated him civilly instead. Regardless, she was a sensitive woman and knew when a man was ogling her, and she didn't *want* him ogling her, not after yesterday.

He couldn't blame her, but he walked to the bunkhouse with his head down and what felt like a fist in his gut.

Supper was uncomfortable. They couldn't quite look each other in the eye. Yesterday felt like a specter in the room with them, much more so this evening than at breakfast when they'd both been dull-witted from the early hour. Throughout the day, they had successfully avoided too much togetherness, but sitting at the same small table with the sun going down seemed to give a whole new meaning to the word. Their attempts at conversation were stilted and uneasy, with both of them eluding any references to yesterday as though they had made some sort of pact to do so.

Finally, when Jude got up to bring some fruit to the table for dessert, she blurted, "Maybe we should talk about it. I mean, if you're going to be here until the fencing is repaired, we can't go on pretending it didn't happen."

Chase did his best to look nonplussed, but it hadn't occurred to him that Jude would force the issue like this. "Uh, guess we can talk, if you want."

Jude sat down with her eyes on her plate. "Well...I suppose there's really nothing to say, but it's difficult to work with someone and watch every word. What I mean is..." Her gaze lifted. "What's wrong with your back?"

"My back?" Chase grinned, weakly. "Where'd that question come from?"

"You don't act like a man with a bad back. Are you on any kind of medication?"

Chase's expression remained rather sickly. "Just...aspirin."

"Why do you lift things if you shouldn't?"

"Like what?"

"Like that heavy sprayer. And...me," she finished in a quiet tone. "You didn't have to lift me yesterday."

Chase's voice dropped, too. "I didn't have to do a lot of what I did yesterday, but that bit of wisdom is in retrospect, Jude. At the time, it didn't seem as though I had a choice."

"We always have choices," she rebutted huskily.

"Do we?" Chase regarded her evenly. "Did you?"

Jude's face flamed. "I know it was my fault!"

"Not entirely. I take responsibility for what I do, Jude, not shunt it off on a woman's shoulders."

"That's . . . noble."

"I'm sorry I hurt you."

Jude dampened her lips. "So you said. I guess I still don't understand what happened." Her gaze fluttered to his. "Do you really have a bad back?"

Chase heaved a long sigh. "If I said no, you'd only have more questions. So, yes, Jude, I have a bad back."

She laughed with some bitterness. "And I still don't know the truth, do I? I'd like *you* to know something, Chase. I'm not any more thrilled about a personal involvement with you than you are with me. But in my case I have no trouble in finding a sound reason for feeling that way. You're not a stable person, and I need stability in the people around me. I've racked my brain to figure out why you got so upset, though, and I'm finally admitting defeat."

"You can't figure me out."

"That's it in a nutshell," Jude conceded. She held up a forefinger. "I'll tell you one thing, though. You're not exactly as you want people to believe." She got to her feet. "I'm going to do the dishes."

Chase's mouth was dry, and he finished his glass of water before getting up from the table. "Supper was good. Thanks."

"You're welcome," Jude said tersely. Chase was almost through the door when she added, "Incidentally, I figured out your trick with Shorty."

"My trick?"

"Or whatever it was. He won't eat until someone says 'okay.'"

Chase managed one more weak grin. "Sorry I teased you about insulting him."

"Well, I shouldn't have said the things I did."

"Did you make friends with Shorty?"

Jude looked him in the eye. "It's easy to make friends with animals, Chase. It's people who turn friendship into something complex."

Chase cleared his throat. "Guess you're right. See you in the morning."

By the following evening, the exterior of the house was finished. Jude never had been able to hold a grudge for long, so she decided to prepare a special dinner to celebrate the end of the painting.

Except for the interior of the house, of course, which seemed like small potatoes after what felt like a hundred gigantic buildings. Without Chase and the trusty sprayer, she would have been painting throughout the summer, so a celebration dinner didn't seem at all out of line.

The day she'd shopped, she'd bought two beautiful steaks, which had been placed in the freezer. Around noon, gleefully seeing the end of paintbrushes, spattered clothing and scarves over her hair, Jude took out the steaks to thaw.

Chase was cleaning the paint canister from the sprayer with the garden hose when she approached him. "Don't be too fussy. Hopefully, I'll never need to use that thing again."

"Never can tell," Chase said. "I'm almost finished."

"Would you do something for me?"

"Sure, name it."

"There's an old charcoal grill in the barn. Would you mind bringing it to the back of the house?"

"Be glad to," Chase said amiably. "Going to grill something?"

"Some steaks I bought the other day." Jude smiled teasingly. "Think you can tolerate an inch-thick T-bone for dinner?"

"Hey, you bet! I'll get that grill right now." Turning off the hose, Chase took off for the barn. He turned and walked backward for a moment. "Have you got charcoal?"

"I bought a bag of that, too. And some lighter fluid," Jude added.

They grinned at each other and went their separate ways; Jude into the house to clean up, Chase to the barn for the grill. He found the creaky old thing and wryly shook his head. It was dirty and rusted and teetering on its three shaky legs.

But he hauled it out of the barn and got busy cleaning it up. For an inch-thick T-bone, he'd do almost anything.

It was such a pleasant evening, Jude set up a card table outside and brought out chairs from the kitchen. A table-cloth and the nicest dishes in the house presented a pretty setting for the meal, and fortunately, the steaks turned out perfectly.

She also served baked potatoes and a tossed salad. Chase savored every bite and told her at least a dozen times how good the food was.

Jude enjoyed the meal, also, although steak wasn't her favorite food. Nevertheless, it was heartwarming to watch Chase's enthusiasm. It was also poignant. They had worked together for days now, and aside from that episode by the creek, had done so harmoniously. Sharing meals created a bond between two people, she had discovered, especially in this isolation where there was no one to focus on but each other.

And yet she suspected that she would have fallen for Chase Sutton if they had met in the middle of a busy city.

She sighed. "Where will you go when you leave here, Chase?"

He looked up from his plate. Was she back to believing his down-on-his-luck-cowpoke persona? Her remark about him being something different than he portrayed had both-ered him ever since. Fixing up this old place was an incred-ibly good cover, should she be so inclined, and hiring a man to help out gave credibility to her presence. But should she have something to hide, she would be watchful and wary, and that remark had hinted at those very qualities.

Yet her expression right now was merely curious, maybe containing a touch of pathos. Chase's heart took a peculiar flip. Would she care when the day came for him to load up and drive away?

For Chase, what had started out as an important but still routine criminal investigation, was now muddied by emotion. Convoluted by the human factor. No way could he have foreseen the present situation, and in all honesty, he didn't know what to do about it.

In answer to Jude's question, he dredged up a vague lie. "I don't have any definite plans. Maybe head for Colorado or Wyoming. There are some pretty good competitions coming up in those states."

"Rodeo," Jude murmured. "What happens when a man gets too old for competition? Or can't compete anymore because of an injury?"

"Uh…" Chase searched his brain. "Probably takes a job on a ranch somewhere."

"Do you have friends who were forced to do that?"

"A few." Returning his attention to his plate, Chase sliced off the last remaining meat on his T-bone. "Best steak I ever ate."

Jude looked over to Shorty, who seemed to be patiently lying in wait. "Can Shorty have the bones?"

"Sure can. Here, Shorty, catch," Chase called, giving the bone a toss.

The pudgy pooch moved with the speed of light and caught the bone in his mouth. Jude laughed. "He's just full of tricks, isn't he?" Her gaze swung to Chase. "A lot like his master."

Chase managed a lopsided grin. "He taught me everything I know."

"Yeah, right," Jude drawled.

*   *   *

With the kitchen back in order, Jude wandered outside. The air was calm and warm, and there was a restlessness in her system that precluded going to bed as early as she'd been doing. Her dress this evening was a faded denim skirt and a sleeveless, print blouse.

The house loomed bright and white in the moonlight. Biscuit followed Jude's slow, ambling stroll toward the corral. Shorty was nowhere to be seen, which wasn't the norm, and Jude peered into the darker shadows to see if he was waiting to dart out and surprise Biscuit.

But she saw nothing of the dog, nor, for that matter, of Chase. The bunkhouse was dark, and she figured that Chase had already gone to bed.

She stopped at the corral, where Thunder came over to the fence. Jude petted the horse's satiny nose and murmured, "You're a pretty thing, Thunder. Maybe someday I'll own a great horse like you."

Chase's voice came out of the shadows. "Where will *you* go when this is over?"

Jude whirled. "I didn't see you. What did you ask me?"

Moving closer, Chase draped his forearms over the corral's top rail. "You asked at supper where I was going when this job was over. I asked you the same question."

"Oh. Well...I'm not sure, either. I don't really have anything in Texas to go back to, except for some furniture. I'll have to get a job, of course."

"In accounting."

"It's what I know."

"You'll have the money from the sale of this place."

"Hopefully. But..."

"And you mentioned some other money coming in," Chase reminded.

It took a moment for Jude to remember her lie. "Uh, yes, I did say that, didn't I? Well, it's not really that certain."

Chase stiffened slightly. "You sounded very certain when you mentioned it before."

Jude was embarrassed. Lies were such damnably bothersome things, and usually returned to haunt a person. Now she wished she hadn't spoken so carelessly, but a confession about inventing a windfall just because she didn't like discussing money—or the lack thereof—would make her look like a fool. And the thought of him remembering her— after he left—as a liar and a fool made her cringe.

"It's...still a p-possibility," she stammered, and felt a wave of humiliation because she had just lied again. She made the whole thing worse by adding, "If it does, it'll just sort of drop out of the sky."

Jude couldn't see it the way they were standing, but Chase's mouth tightened into a thin, hard line. "Like, maybe," he said through clenched teeth, "you might win a lottery."

"A lottery in Nevada?" Jude said with a forced laugh, hoping to change the subject. "Is the state going to allow a lottery? I hadn't heard."

"I doubt it," Chase said brusquely, wanting to get back to that drop-from-the-sky comment of Jude's. It was a thin connection to his quest here, but why in hell would she phrase herself that way?

Jude stayed one step ahead of him by sighing. "Gosh, it's a beautiful night. Look at all those stars."

It was a night perfect for romance. The sky looked like black velvet shot throughout with sparkling sequins. A sliver of a moon appeared as fragile and hung by invisible strings. Chase took a long look and thought about the mysteries of life, and why one particular woman should suddenly become important to a man.

His gaze dropped from the heavenly sight to Jude, who looked just as heavenly in the moonlight. She stirred him as no woman ever had. Why her? Why not any one of the multitude of other women who had passed through his life?

Groaning, he laid his head down on his arms, which were still atop the corral rail. Jude sent him a sharp glance. "Is something wrong?" When he didn't answer, she raised her hand to his arm. "Chase?"

Her touch sent a lightning bolt of awareness through his body. He suddenly felt trapped, locked into a scenario he despised, frustrated by ethics and standards and longtime practices.

From his obvious misery, Jude knew positively that something deep and dark and sinister was eating at him. Her imagination took her from a fatal disease to Chase being on the FBI's most wanted list. Her fearful heartbeat felt smothering. "Chase, what is it?" she questioned in an unsteady voice. "You can talk to me. Sometimes it relieves the pressure to talk to someone about a problem."

He had to stifle another groan, but it welled in his throat and threatened to choke him.

"I can see how unhappy you are," Jude whispered.

"Honey, you don't know the half of it," he said raggedly, and straightened.

Compassion struck Jude in massive waves. "Oh, Chase," she whispered while wrapping her arms around his waist and laying her cheek on his chest.

The embrace was so unexpected, Chase nearly lost his balance. He reacted automatically, locking his arms around her to regain his equilibrium. And then, she felt so good he just stood there and basked in the sensation.

"You can tell me what's bothering you," Jude whispered. His scent was making her dizzy. Or something was. She certainly hadn't intended anything sexual by this embrace, but a primeval need was seeping into her senses. Chase aroused her so easily, but this time she hadn't been looking for any such foolishness between them, and it struck her as sad that she had so little self-control with him.

Chase was deliberately trying not to think about anything. Holding Jude in the moonlight had become crucial to life itself. He couldn't make love to her again, he knew that. But accepting a compassionate embrace from a woman wasn't a crime in anybody's book.

Jude was attempting sanity at this strangely insane moment. She had vowed to avoid any further physical involvement with Chase, and she herself had instigated it again. There was response in Chase's arms, in his body, and one false move from her would have them seeking a bed.

Pursuing their previous subject was her only recourse. Her voice was barely perceptible as she posed a difficult question. "Chase...are...are you wanted by the law?"

He couldn't quite make out her words, but verbal communication had lost significance. He stirred slightly, moving his body against hers, and placed his lips in her hair, closing his eyes in the process, absorbing her essence through touch and smell.

"Did you hear what I said?" Jude whispered.

He said nothing, but reached down between them. She heard the rasp of his zipper, and felt her skirt being raised. Her panties were shoved down, and breathlessly, too excited to speak, she helped him find his goal.

He lifted her. "Put your legs around me."

It didn't seem possible that he was inside her so quickly. With her lips parted, she looked into his eyes. Once had not been enough for either of them. Her tongue flicked to moisten her lips only a heartbeat before his mouth hungrily covered hers.

Guilt made Chase rough. His mouth was bruising, the thrusts of his hips hard and angry. The anger was for himself, not for Jude. She made him want to weep, another emotion with which he had precious little experience. She made him want to love her into eternity, and in their case, eternity might last only another hour, another day.

But Jude interpreted his roughness as passion. She felt him lean against a corral post and lift her higher. Her mind was spinning, everything was wild, tempestuous sensation.

Chase held off completion until he heard her cries and felt the final demands of her body, then he let himself go and nearly lost his footing.

Breathing hard, he felt reality returning. His arms and legs were weak. His physical satisfaction was tainted by guilt. Grimly he untangled their bodies and let Jude's feet slide to the ground. She teetered against him, and he held her until she had calmed.

She moved first, lifting her face to see his. Moonlight reflected on the tears on her cheeks. Chase studied her for a long moment, wishing to God he knew what to say now.

"You're sorry again," Jude said sadly.

"Do you want me to lie, Jude?"

"I should hate you," she whispered brokenly. "Please let go of me."

When he obeyed, she backed up a step. He turned away to straighten his clothing. Spying her panties on the ground, she bent to retrieve them, tucking them into a pocket of her skirt.

There was nothing to say, she realized, looking at his broad back. She had asked for trouble again, and he'd given it to her. Without love or affection or kindness. Even more painful to face, she couldn't hate him.

"Good night," she managed to say as she started for the house.

"Jude!"

She stopped and turned. "What?"

"What did you ask me before?"

She thought for a moment, then recalled the question. "I asked if you were wanted by the law," she said dully.

"If I were wanted by the law?" Chase repeated incredulously. "Is that what you think?"

"It's not so farfetched. You're keeping something bottled up. Maybe someday you'll be able to open up with a woman. I feel . . . bad that she won't be me. Good night, Chase."

Nine

Jude awakened in the night to ponder telling Chase to leave in the morning. The painting, other than the interior of the house, was finished, and the fencing didn't really have to be repaired, although, unquestionably, good solid fence lines would up the value of the ranch.

The night quiet played on Jude's nerves, leading her into questions about herself. She behaved like a person with no morals at all, or a woman without a will around Chase, and she was neither. Or she hadn't been. What she was now, other than a sucker for vivid blue eyes and more sex appeal than any man deserved, wasn't clear. Her intellect said, *Kick him out of your life. Do it now!* But every female instinct she possessed leaned toward maintaining the relationship for as long as possible. Her female instincts weren't exactly rational where Chase was concerned, Jude realized, but kicking him out of her life would be so final, and she wasn't ready for "final" with him.

All right, Colter, where do you want this to go? Do you think Chase is going to do an abrupt turnabout and suddenly become Mr. Open and Honest?

But then, she hadn't been completely honest with him, either. Why did her stupid lie about money coming in keep popping up? The only definite money in her future, other than the "someday" proceeds from the sale of the ranch, was the cash she had withdrawn from her savings account.

But why, pray tell, was Chase so interested in her financial situation? He talked about money an awful lot, didn't he?

She needed to figure him out with the most driving desperation of her adult years. For her own peace of mind, maybe to prove to herself that she hadn't become a complete fool, she had to learn the secret that seemed to be tearing him apart. It was obvious that their attraction was mutual, and there had to be a reason why he kept fighting it so hard.

No, she wouldn't—*couldn't*—tell him to leave. It was odd that he didn't leave on his own, given the enormous regret he suffered whenever he crossed the line with her.

But one thing was crystal clear. There was nothing wrong with Chase's back. Only a man with a remarkably *strong* back could have performed the way he had tonight.

Jude wasn't at peace when she fell asleep again, but at least she had made a decision. Until the work was finished on the ranch, she would not disturb the status quo. Maybe by then she would be rid of this frustrating infatuation for her hired man.

"Would you mind using your truck to do an errand for me this morning?"

Chase raised his sleepy eyes from his bowl of oatmeal. He'd put in a restless, guilt-ridden night, and it took every ounce of strength in his traitorous system to look directly at Jude this morning. "What's the errand?"

"Pick up some new fence posts at the Naples hardware store."

"No problem," Chase mumbled.

"Thank you." Jude pulled some cash out of the pocket of her jeans. "I'm not sure how many you can buy with this, but get all you can."

Chase stared at the money. "Aren't you coming with me?"

"No. I want to get started on the inside of the house. All the curtains and shades have to be taken down before the rooms are painted. There's a lot of junk to sort through, too, a lot to throw away."

The bills in Jude's hand—at least two hundred dollars—held Chase's gaze, probably because he wasn't up to direct eye contact with her. Her trust bothered him, irritated him, actually. "How do you know I won't blow your money on something else?"

"Will you?"

"If I'd do that, it wouldn't bother me much to lie about it, would it?"

"Are you trying to pick a fight, Chase? Would you rather I didn't trust you?"

Chase took a look at his bowl of cereal and grimaced. "I hate oatmeal."

"Well, that makes a lot of sense," Jude said grumpily. "Look, if you don't want to go to Naples, just say so. I'm sure I can make other arrangements."

"Did I say I wouldn't go?" Chase got to his feet. "I'll go right now."

"Finish your breakfast first. The hardware store doesn't open until eight."

"Thanks, but I'm not hungry."

Ignoring his petulant tone, Jude held out the money. "If you don't mind, I'd like you to price barbed wire, too. I think what's out there merely needs tightening, but we may have to do some replacing in spots."

"Do you have a wire stretcher?"

"A what?"

"It's a tool used to tighten barbed wire," Chase explained.

"Oh. Well, I don't know. Did you see one in the toolshed?"

"Not that I remember. I'll look around before I go." Chase plucked the bills from her hand without touching it and tucked them into his pocket. He left the kitchen in a hurry, glad to escape Jude, whose proximity magnified his guilt to an unbearable level.

With Shorty on his heels, Chase went directly to the musty toolshed and began sorting through its mishmash of tools and junk. No wire stretcher. Looking around, he spied a pile he hadn't gone through before. Tossing some of the junk aside, he came upon a heavy canvas bag. It was securely strapped closed, but from its bulk and configuration, clearly contained something.

Doubting that it held anything of any importance, Chase nevertheless unbuckled the straps. He pushed the top of the bag back and then stood there in shock. The bag was full of money. Neatly bundled greenbacks.

He took out one of the bundles and fanned the bills—all twenties. Some of the bundles, he discovered upon examination, were hundreds, some were fifties. There were thousands of dollars in the old canvas bag, and Chase's knees suddenly felt like wet noodles.

He cussed, quietly but passionately. It had to be drug money. Why else would it be hidden under a pile of junk?

But why would Jude send him out here to poke around if she knew about it?

He thought of toting the bag into the house and point-blank asking Jude about it. Questioning her. Grilling her, if need be. Getting to the bottom of this mess once and for all.

But laying his cards out that distinctly would be his final hand. The publicity of a narcotics agent on the premises would bring everything to a screeching halt. Certainly the impending drug shipment would be aborted.

Assuming that Jude was involved, of course. If she wasn't . . . ? What if everything she'd told him about living in Texas and only coming here to sell the ranch was true? What if she knew absolutely nothing about this bag of money?

But what about the windfall she'd mentioned? Damn it, did she know about this canvas bag or didn't she? And if she did, why was she so cautious about spending money?

It didn't make sense, not any of it. Grimly, Chase re-buckled the straps on the bag and put it back where he'd found it. He piled the junk on top of it again, flinching when he thought of how easily this greasy old building could go up in flames.

But he didn't want to move the money to a safer place. It could belong to someone—Jude?—and that person could come looking for it.

Forcing himself to search for the nonexistent wire stretcher again, Chase finally gave up and left the toolshed. But walking away from it, toward his pickup, he glanced back at the building with a scowl and a muttered curse. Every time he almost reached the point of believing Jude innocent of the whole sordid affair, something else happened to make him doubt again.

He had to stick to his original plan. And he had to keep his hands off of Jude.

From the kitchen window, Jude watched Shorty jump up into the pickup and Chase seat himself behind the wheel. Apparently he hadn't found the tool he'd mentioned, but if they really needed the thing to repair the fences, she could probably borrow or rent one from Sam Shelton.

The truck's engine popped, backfired and finally rattled to life, and Jude sighed when it eventually got going and disappeared down the road. Chase's misery this morning had been completely obvious. Why in heaven's name was he hanging around? He could earn twice, three times as much wage as she was paying him, just by driving a short distance to any of the several mining operations in the area.

Oh, yes, he'd mentioned disliking mines and chemicals. But Jude couldn't help feeling that Chase's determination to stick it out had something to do with her.

Their relationship had to be the strangest ever. Twice they had made unbelievably passionate love. Most couples in their situation would be billing and cooing all over the place. Instead, they grumped at each other over the breakfast table and avoided honesty as though it would bring the roof down around their heads.

But mornings were not the best time for either of them. Jude sighed. Maybe by this afternoon Chase would be grinning again. She hoped so.

Chase parked the pickup next to Jude's car and got out. Shorty leapt from the floor of the truck and landed on the ground as he always did, nearly upside down.

"Good thing I didn't name you Grace," Chase drawled.

Jude came out of the house. "You got a pretty good load." She walked to the back of the pickup to inspect the new fence posts.

"Do you want them unloaded?"

Jude frowned. "Well...I'm not sure what to do with them. What's the best way to proceed with the fence repairs?"

Chase thought about it. "It would probably make the best sense to drop them where they're needed."

"Out along the fence line?" Jude's face brightened. "Yes, of course, that's what we'll do."

"I can do it."

"I'll help," Jude insisted. "I'm done in the house for now, anyway."

Chase eyed a big stack of rubble next to the back door of the house. "Did you get all of that from inside the house?"

Jude nodded. "I have to find out if there's a place in the area to get rid of it. It's mostly old newspapers and magazines. Uncle Simon must have saved everything."

"You didn't know him very well, did you?"

"Not at all, actually. Him and Mom were never close, outside of exchanging Christmas cards with impersonal messages. Mom never said it right out, but I grew up with the impression that she wasn't sorry to leave Nevada." Jude shrugged. "I don't know. Maybe she didn't like my father's brother. At any rate, he never came to Texas to see us and we never returned to Nevada to see him."

"Yet he left you this ranch."

"My father left me this ranch, Chase. With the understanding that his brother could live out his life on it."

Chase's eyes narrowed. "You said your mother didn't have much in the way of assets. Didn't she ever try to break your father's will so *she* could sell the ranch?"

"My mother was an honorable woman who loved her husband very much. To my knowledge, she never once tried to alter the terms of Dad's will. Besides, I think Dad believed she would stay here."

"Instead, she took you and went to Texas."

"To her own family, yes." Jude eyed the fence posts again. "I've got an idea. Why don't I drive the pickup and you throw off the posts whenever you see a spot in the fence that needs a new one?"

"Makes sense," Chase agreed.

Jude's gaze moved to him. "Want some lunch first?"

"I grabbed a burger in town."

"Then we might as well get to it, all right?"

"Might as well."

Jude opened the door of the pickup and sat behind the wheel. "Oh, it has a regular shift." Actually, what the old truck had was an awful-looking thing sticking out of the floor. "How old is this pickup, anyway?"

"It's a '63."

"Practically an antique," Jude commented.

Chase laid his forearm over the door and peered in at her. "Do you know how to drive a straight stick?"

"Uh, sure."

"You don't sound very confident."

"Well…it's been a while. But I'm sure it'll come back in two shakes."

Shorty slithered around Chase's legs and hopped up to prop his front paws on the narrow running board. "He's afraid of the truck leaving without him," Chase said.

"He can ride along," Jude told him. "Come on, Shorty. You can come with us." In the next instant, with Shorty clambering over her legs, Jude laughed. "You sure can move fast when you want to, Shorty."

"Move over," Chase instructed. "I'll drive us out to the pasture."

"All right," Jude said agreeably, and slid over on the seat. But she couldn't slide very far, not with Shorty's round, firmly packed little body taking up its fair share of the seat.

When Chase got in, he found himself up against Jude. His breath caught. "Uh, can't you get over a little more?"

Jude smiled sweetly. "Not unless I push Shorty out the other door." Chase's face was mere inches from hers, and she thoroughly enjoyed the way his features tensed when she deliberately and slowly licked her lips.

He turned away and slammed the door shut with a sharply stated, "Stop it, Jude."

"Stop what?" she innocently inquired.

"You know damn well what you just did."

She moved her shoulder against his arm. "That?"

"No, not that. I meant what you did with your tongue."
Chase started the motor and revved the rattling engine with
several hard pumps of the gas pedal.

"You mean, I shouldn't lick my lips where you might see
it?"

"Don't lick anything, goddamn it!"

Jude couldn't hold back her laughter any longer, and
Chase's glowering look only made her laugh all the harder.

"I'm glad you're getting such a bang out of me," Chase
snapped.

"Oh, stop being such an old stick in the mud," Jude said
as she wiped her eyes. "For someone who started out teasing me every chance he got, you're turning into an awful
grouch."

"And we both know why, don't we?"

"I didn't seduce you last night, Chase. The first time
might have been my doing, but last night was yours."

The pickup was moving through the compound. "Who
hugged who last night?" Chase inquired sarcastically.

"A hug of simple kindness is not a prelude to seduction,
my friend," Jude replied in an equally sarcastic tone. "At
least, it never was with anyone else."

Chase slammed on the brakes, put the car in Park, turned
in the seat and clasped Jude by the back of the head. His
eyes were dark and burning, his jaw clenched. "You're
making me crazy." His mouth covered hers in a hard kiss of
utter possession. Jude whimpered deep in her throat and
opened her mouth for his tongue.

The kiss lasted until Chase raised his head. Jude's lips
were wet and trembling. Her breathing was erratic, making
her breasts rise and fall. He stared, his gaze roaming from
her flushed face to her heaving chest.

"Did...you prove something to yourself?" Jude asked
hoarsely.

"Maybe I did."

"A cop-out if I ever heard one. Would you like to hear what it proved to me?"

"No." With his jaw tightly clenched again, Chase let loose of her and put his hands on the steering wheel. He was so tense that he gave the engine too much gas, and the pickup leapt forward and died. Angrily he started the motor again.

Jude kept her head tilted to watch him while he drove, not caring if he liked it or not. She was pressed up against him, closer than she had to be, but she'd be damned if she would move over.

"Getting your eyes full?" Chase finally muttered.

"Plenty full. Did you know that your lower lip protrudes when you pout?"

"I'm not pouting, damn it!"

"Of course you're pouting," Jude replied almost soothingly. A devilish impulse made her reach up and touch his sexy bottom lip. "That's a pout if I ever saw one."

Chase jerked his head back. "Jude, that's enough!"

She wanted to crawl onto his lap. Actually, she wanted to unzip his jeans and *then* crawl onto his lap. His comment about her making him crazy was only part of the story; what he did to her would be x-rated in any theater.

A wistful sigh escaped as Jude laid her head on Chase's upper arm. She ignored his wince and asked softly, "When the work's all done here, will you just say goodbye and drive away, Chase?"

He resorted to emotional cruelty. "That's my plan, yes."

"I don't believe you. Something's happening with us, and I don't think you'll be able to forget it any easier than I will."

He made a sound somewhere in between a choked growl and a cough. "Think what you want."

"I know you want me right now."

"Maybe I do, but I'm not going to do anything about it." They had reached the fence line, and Chase stopped the truck. "Here's where I get out."

Jude lifted her head, but he wouldn't look at her. "I behave differently with you than with any other man, Chase," she said quietly. "I want you to know that. I've never been aggressive before, but you turn something loose inside me, something I didn't even know was there. What do you suppose it is?"

"Hormones," Chase growled, and opened the door. He stood outside and rubbed his mouth, so torn up he wondered how much longer he could continue this charade.

Sighing, Jude slid over to occupy the driver's space. In the side mirror on the door, she watched Chase climb into the back of the pickup.

"I'm ready," he called. "Drive slow."

"Right." Jude eyed the ghastly shifting lever, then the two pedals next to the gas pedal on the floor. "The brake's the one on the right," she decided, muttering to herself. Which meant that the other was the clutch. It had been years since she'd driven a vehicle with a clutch, and she'd only done it then a few times.

She stuck her left foot out to the clutch pedal and realized she couldn't quite reach it. "Can this seat be adjusted?" she called through the open window.

The question struck Chase right between the eyes. This old pickup was almost as foreign to him as it was to Jude. It was, after all, a loaner from the police department's motor pool. So was the horse trailer. Both had been confiscated by officers in the line of duty and would go on the auction block at the city's next sale.

"Uh, let me check." Jumping to the ground, Chase opened the door and felt around under the seat, hoping that Jude wouldn't catch on to his ignorance. Relieved to locate a lever, he adjusted it and gave the seat a yank forward.

Jude was smiling. Chase's face was close enough to kiss, and when the seat suddenly leapt forward, she was thrown against him. "That's much better," she purred.

He jumped back as though scorched. "Can you reach the pedals better now?" he questioned raggedly.

"Oh, that, too," Jude sang out.

Shaking his head, Chase climbed back into the bed of the truck.

"Chase?" Jude was frowning at the shift lever.

"What?"

"Which way do I go with the shift to find low."

"I thought you knew how to drive a stick shift," he said irately.

"I do, but this old thing—"

"Low is to the left and up," Chase interrupted.

Jude nodded. "Thanks." She pushed on the clutch and started maneuvering the shift. It made an awful noise. "Should it be doing that?" she called.

"You're grinding the gears. Push the clutch all the way to the floor."

Finally Jude located what she thought was low gear. She was all set, with her hands on the wheel and her gaze out the windshield. Only when she released the clutch, the pickup shot forward and the motor died.

An urge to giggle welled in her throat. She glanced at Shorty, who seemed to be sitting there with his toenails burrowed into the seat, and the urge became worse.

Chase wearily called, "Let the clutch out slowly."

"I thought I did." She restarted the engine, pushed in the clutch, released it with more caution, and the pickup jerked forward a few feet. Jude slammed on the brake and the clutch at the same time, then released both to jerk forward again.

Chase was hanging on and swearing under his breath. "Damn it, woman, are you trying to kill me?"

It was too much. The laughter nearly choking Jude came gushing out, and she pushed both pedals again and laid her head on her arms on the steering wheel.

"Jude?"

She tried to stifle her giggling, but tears were running down her cheeks. "Just . . . a minute," she croaked.

"What're you doing? Damn it, let's get this show on the road!" Bending over, Chase peered into the back window of the cab. Jude's head was down on her arms and her shoulders were shaking. His stomach turned over, because it was obvious she was crying.

"Aw, hell," he muttered. Positive that his gruff remarks had hurt her feelings, he hopped over the side of the pickup to the ground. This time his landing was a little awkward and he felt a pain shoot through his left ankle. Ignoring it, he opened the door and bent over to peer in. "Jude? I'm sorry, honey. Don't cry. We'll work things out, I promise. Just don't cry, okay?"

Astonished, Jude lifted her head. "You *do* care how I feel!"

Chase's features darkened. "You haven't been crying, you've been laughing!"

"Well, of course I've been laughing," Jude said with utter logic only a second before another burst of giggles erupted. "Oh, Chase, this is the funniest thing I've ever seen. Shorty's got his toenails dug into the seat, and . . ."

Furious, Chase slammed the door shut. His ankle refused to be ignored any longer and hurt like hell. But he climbed back into the bed of the truck, yelling, "When you're through playing around, I'd like to get this job done."

Jude stuck her head out the window. "If you hadn't turned into such an intractable grump, you'd be laughing, too." She settled herself behind the wheel again, muttering under her breath, "All right, Colter, release the clutch slowly."

* * *

Once Jude understood the old truck's quirks, she handled it just fine. She followed the crude roads along the fence lines, and whenever Chase or she spotted a badly rotted post, she stopped so he could throw off a new one.

The bed of the pickup was empty before they had covered all of the fencing, however, which bothered Jude. But she had no more extra money to spend on fence posts. Her little remaining cash had to be stretched until she paid Chase's wages, found another job and went back to work. As it was, only a miracle would see her through another move and the weeks, at the very least, it would take her after that to earn a paycheck.

She was considering giving Reno a try, although she had no assurances that Chase ever went near his hometown. But going anywhere else would guarantee never seeing him again, and she wasn't ready to give up on Chase.

With the last new post lying by the side of the road, Jude waited for Chase to get down from the truck bed and into the cab. She realized, when he climbed in on the passenger side with a wince, that he had hurt himself.

Instantly she had second thoughts about that conclusion she'd reached regarding his back. "Are you in pain?"

"I twisted my ankle."

"Your ankle! I thought you had hurt your back."

Chase shoved Shorty over a little more. "My back's fine."

"That's exactly what I figured," Jude said with some spirit. "Why did you concoct that story about a back injury?"

"I don't want to talk about it."

Jude got the truck moving and sent Chase a glance. "You're certainly in a foul mood today."

"Baby, you don't know the half of it," Chase muttered.

"If making love with me leaves such a bitter aftertaste, why do you do it?"

Chase cast her a dourful look. "Good question, Jude. *Real* good question."

"Well, at least you didn't say it was because I was easy," she said in a small voice.

"I don't think of you that way."

"Maybe not, but that's what I've been. You can cheer up, Chase. I promise to be very, very difficult in the future. And cold. Does that make you feel any better?"

Chase turned his face to the side window. "Yeah, it helps a lot."

He'd spoken cynically, and Jude felt an uncharacteristic rise of anger. "Let's keep this in perspective, Chase. I'm to blame for a lot of what's happened, but not all of it."

"Did I say you were?"

"You implied . . ."

Chase's head jerked around. "I implied nothing. Listen, when we get to the house, I'm going to drop you off and pick up some tools. Then I'm coming back out here to start on the fence repairs, and I want to work alone."

"Without me."

"You got it."

Jude's anger got stronger. "Well, that's fine with me. If you think I've been enjoying your bad humor today, you've got another thought coming."

"Fine. We understand each other."

"Perfectly," Jude said crisply, which was a barefaced lie. She might never understand Chase Sutton, not if it took ten years to repair the damn fence!

Ten

It was late when Chase quit working on the fences for the day and arrived back at the compound. As Jude had been watching for him, she went to the back door and called, "Chase, supper's ready."

"I'll be up after I shower."

Jude frowned as she watched Chase walk to the bunkhouse. "You're limping!"

"It's nothing."

His macho attitude exasperated Jude. "Chase, come up here and let me look at that ankle."

"After I shower."

She fumed as he limped on to the bunkhouse. "Of all the stubborn, irritating..."

Actually, she had done quite a bit of fuming that afternoon. Her and Chase's relationship was taking a discomfiting swing to emotions she would rather not ruffle. Like anger, for instance. And waspishness. Were they reacting to the frustration of confusion by lashing out at each other?

If Chase would talk to her in a straightforward manner they could iron out any problem, Jude felt. But how did a woman get a man to open up if he had an aversion to doing so?

Jude put supper on hold; before they ate, she was going to examine Chase's ankle whether he liked it or not. He'd been injured on the job, after all, and if he needed medical attention, it was her responsibility.

He finally came in, wearing clean clothes and looking damp and fresh from his shower.

"Sit down and take off your boot, please," Jude requested.

The only reason Chase complied was because he knew his ankle needed wrapping and he had none. Carefully he slid the boot from his foot, then his sock.

Jude knelt on the floor and took his foot on her lap. "It's swollen and discolored. How did it happen?"

"When I jumped off the truck," Chase said tonelessly, wanting to keep this as impersonal as possible. Jude's fingers gently probing the injured area of his ankle was putting that bit of common sense to the test, however. The ceiling light was on and reflecting in her hair, and whatever scent she was wearing was wafting upward. Chase tried not to breathe it in.

"Well, I don't think it's serious, but it does need wrapping," Jude said matter-of-factly. "Sit here and I'll see what I can find."

While she was gone, Chase tiredly leaned his elbow on the table and put his head in his hand. He thought about the money in that canvas bag in the toolshed. He thought about his mission on the Colter Ranch, and of how far he'd gone over the line with a suspect. Twice. Worse, he thought of how badly he'd like to cross that same line again. Jude was in his blood, stirring it relentlessly. How was he going to maintain a level head until this thing was finally over?

Jude came back. "I found it," she exclaimed, waving a roll of elasticized bandage. "I thought I had brought it along, but I wasn't sure where it was." She kneeled in front of Chase again.

"I can put it on, Jude."

She smiled up at him. "But I can do it better. Relax, Chase, this isn't a pass."

He wished it were. He wished he could take her by the arms and urge her up and onto his lap, into his arms. Through narrowed eyes, he watched her wind the tan-colored bandage around and around his ankle.

Jude noticed the slight trembling of her hands. Touching Chase for whatever reason was no trivial matter. Drifter or not, he was an overwhelming man. Or he was to her, however he might affect other people.

"There, all done," she said brightly, getting to her feet. "Now we can eat. It's all ready." Quickly Jude brought the food to the table. Tonight's fare was vegetarian stew, and she could see Chase giving the dish a questioning once-over.

She made no comment about it and joined him at the table. They filled their plates and began eating.

"Did you accomplish very much with the fencing?" Jude asked.

"Got about half a dozen posts replaced. I'm going to need a wire stretcher."

"I'll see that you have one." With his fork, Chase was cutting chunks of carrots, rutabagas and potatoes into smaller pieces. Jude watched for a moment. "You're not fond of supper tonight, are you?"

"It would be great with a little meat."

"It's a healthy meal, Chase. Have some salad."

He eyed the salad bowl. "Thanks."

"How long do you think it will take to complete the fence repairs?" Jude inquired.

Chase had been anticipating that question. "Quite a while if it's done right." His eyes met Jude's. "How long do you want it to take?"

She thought the word *forever,* but suspecting what he was getting at, said, "I can afford to pay you for another week. Will that be long enough?"

The thought of that canvas bag in the toolshed tautened Chase's features. "Tell you what. I'd like to leave here knowing I did the best job possible. If you run out of money before the fence is done, I'll finish it for nothing."

Jude stiffened. "No, absolutely not. Thank you for the offer, but . . . no."

Her refusal surprised Chase. Did she really have so much pride that she would refuse a few days of free labor?

Or was one more week all she wanted him to remain on the ranch?

Actually, this case was dragging out longer than he'd hoped at its inception. He wasn't comfortable with either doubting or believing Jude and, for that matter, his own behavior was just about the most *un*comfortable guilt trip he'd ever experienced.

He cleaned his plate quickly, refused seconds and got up from the table. "Good night, Jude. See you in the morning."

"Good night, Chase," she said softly. Alone then, Jude admitted that she was as close to a broken heart as any woman could get. What's more, her ordinary gumption had deserted her when she needed it most. Her pride, however—the little she still possessed—was beginning to rebel. Accept Chase's hard work without paying for it? Not on a bet.

The day of separation for the two of them wasn't very far away, and nothing was going to change, Jude realized with sudden sad certainty, not with her, not with Chase. She felt a stinging behind her eyes, and got up to clear the table to forestall the threatening self-pity.

* * *

Two nights later Chase awakened to Shorty's howls. Chase jumped out of bed and yanked on his jeans. He stepped on his bare left foot too hard and received a sharp reminder that his ankle was still tender. Quickly he sat on the edge of the bed and pulled on his socks and boots. The ankle felt better with the support of the boot, and Chase stood up to grab his shirt.

Stepping outside, Chase stopped to listen and look around. Shorty was somewhere behind the barn, setting up an awful ruckus. Instead of calling out and telling Shorty to quiet down, Chase went to find him.

On the back side of the barn, Chase approached his pet. Shorty instantly began wriggling and whimpering, obviously delighted to see his best friend and master in the middle of the night. Chase hunkered down and scratched Shorty's ears. "What's all the noise about, old fellow?"

Jude, in her robe and slippers, came dashing around the barn. "Why was he howling again?"

Chase was looking off into the black night. "Maybe because of that light out there."

"What light?" Jude turned. "Why…there is a light. But it must be a mile off. What do you suppose it is?"

The light was diffused and ill-defined, appearing almost ghostlike. It was, however, precisely within the vicinity of the hills in which the landing strip was located. Chase's pulse was hard but steady. This was it. He could feel it in his bones. He stood and peered in the dark at Jude's face, which was still aimed at the mysterious light.

"You don't have any idea what's making that light?"

"No. Do you?" Jude's hand lifted to her own face, where she touched her lips in a troubled gesture. "Could it be a fire? Oh, Chase, what if it's a fire?"

There was no time for a long conversation. Chase knew if he was going to intercept the plane and the pickup person or persons, he had to get going.

But something was finally, irrevocably seeping into his senses: Jude had no knowledge of that landing strip's criminal usage. Whatever was taking place on her land this night was totally beyond her ken.

"Go back to the house and stay there," he said gruffly.

"Pardon?" Jude's startled gaze swung Chase's way.

"I've got something to do. I'll see you later." Practically running, Chase returned to the bunkhouse for his gun and truck keys.

Perplexed, Jude followed. When Chase came running back outside, she tried to stop him. "Chase, where are you going? And why? It's after midnight."

"I know what time it is. Stay here, Jude. And turn out that light in your bedroom. Keep everything dark."

She was too stunned to react quickly, and stood there while he ran to his truck, started it and drove off with such haste the pickup's tires spun in the dirt. "Turn on the headlights," she shouted.

But the dark truck kept going...without headlights...heading into the heart of Colter land.

"This is crazy," Jude mumbled. If that light was a fire, didn't it make better sense to drive to a phone and request help?

But Chase wasn't acting as if he thought a fire had somehow gotten started on Colter land. There was something else happening, and it had him alarmed and driving away in the dark. And ordering her to turn out the house lights.

In the next instant life returned to Jude's benumbed senses and she ran for the house. Breathing hard, she took the stairs two at a time, tearing off her robe as she went. In her bedroom she switched off the light and shed her nightgown. Within three minutes, wearing jeans and the blouse she'd had on earlier, and with her car keys in her hand, she retraced her steps to the first floor.

Outside, the stillness of the night stopped her. She cocked her head and picked up the distant sound of Chase's truck, then ran for her car. She had driven beyond the barn before she hesitated again. The old fence line roads were in horrible condition. By driving her nice car on them, she would be risking her one major asset.

But something was terribly wrong. Chase had either lost his mind or that light meant something to him that she couldn't grasp. One thing she felt by instinct alone: he was heading into some kind of danger.

Jude shivered and stepped on the gas pedal. The road was precarious enough with light; without it, she hit every pothole and rut. There were choices along the way, but she had a general idea of the location of that light and kept on the right track.

Chase cut the engine and coasted to the bottom of a long hill. From way under the seat he retrieved three sets of handcuffs and attached them to his belt. Unscrewing the overhead light bulb and exiting the truck silently, he let the door hang open and began walking. He patted the loaded gun in his belt and the extra cartridges in his pocket. Thoughts of Jude and the injustice he'd done her attempted to badger him, but he pushed them aside to concentrate on the job at hand. He would think about Jude when this was over, and wonder then how he could make her understand.

Reaching the crest of the hill after a lengthy hike, Chase crouched behind a patch of sagebrush and felt a sudden burst of adrenaline. At the north end of the landing strip was a parked car. Its headlights were beamed on the field, obviously providing light for the plane to land.

Chase listened and heard music, a radio. Whoever was waiting for the plane wasn't worried about discovery. Chase studied the scene of bright light and black shadows, and finally decided that only one person was down there. Unless there was someone inside the car.

He had to get closer. He had to be ready to move in when the plane was down and immediately after the exchange of drugs and money. The person below was rather nonchalantly leaning against the right front fender of his vehicle, and it occurred to Chase that the man or woman had done this before and still believed wholeheartedly that no one lived on the Colter Ranch.

Dropping below the visibility line of the hilltop, Chase began walking in a wide circle with the intention of coming up on the thug's blind side.

With her eyes squinted and straining to see in the dark, Jude spotted Chase's pickup with an immense sigh of relief.

But he was nowhere to be seen. A sixth sense told her to move quietly and invisibly, and she turned off the ignition and then frowned at the still dark ceiling light. The second she opened the door it would come on, and just how could she prevent that from happening?

Gingerly she fiddled with the plastic cover on the light and finally felt it giving. It dropped to the seat and Jude left it there. Feeling around with her fingers, she found one tiny bulb, which came out of the socket easily enough.

Quite proud of her ingenuity, Jude cautiously opened the door and stepped outside. The door of Chase's pickup was hanging open, so she left hers the same way. She stopped then, frowning over what sounded like faraway music.

What is going on out here? she thought rather frantically. Surely Chase hadn't gone flying off into the dark night without headlights just because some kids had chosen Colter land to hold a beer bust.

But there weren't any voices or laughter. In fact, other than the distant music, there weren't any sounds at all.

Where was Chase? Obviously the light and faint music were coming from over that hill. Was that where Chase had gone?

Jude looked at the long, dark, gradually ascending hill ahead of her. Wasn't that the spot where Chase had asked her what she thought of the landing strip in the field below?

The landing strip and Chase's odd reluctance to leave the ranch began to make some kind of crazy sense to Jude. Or, at least, the two diverse subjects seemed eerily connected.

Suddenly, from out of the black night, the sound of a plane reached Jude's ears. She looked for it, squinting at the sky, and realized uneasily that the plane, wherever it was, was flying without lights.

But it was going to land. Positive of that much, at least, Jude began running up the long hill. With her heart pounding, she gained the crest just as the plane swooped out of the darkness and touched down onto the crude landing strip.

Its motor was cut almost instantly. Crouching behind some brush, Jude watched it come to a nearly silent halt within the bright headlights of the car. Then the headlights went out and everything was suddenly as black as ink below. Jude blinked and strained to see. There was only silence for a few minutes, then a laugh. Next she heard some voices, an angry shout, a curse.

"Ohmygod," she whispered, certain that Chase was right in the middle of whatever was happening.

But what *was* happening? She stood, as though standing would improve her vision. She wanted to call Chase's name, to shriek it into the darkness. But she was afraid to do anything that might put him in jeopardy.

And then she remembered that he had willingly put himself down there, when whatever was going on was none of his business.

A frisson of dread chilled Jude's spine. Chase had been waiting for this. That unlighted plane dropping onto Colter land in the middle of the night was why he had taken her handyman's job, why he had agreed to work for her low wage, and why he had stayed when it had been so obvious that he would have preferred leaving.

His dissimulation hadn't been about her at all. She'd been a handy and willing female, nothing more. And to his credit, he had even fabricated a story about a back injury to avoid...to avoid... Jude forced herself to face the awful truth. *To avoid making love to her.*

The greatest humiliation of her life nearly brought her to her knees. She was about to run back to her car and get away from there before Chase could discover her presence, when the headlights of the vehicle at the landing strip flashed on again.

Startled, Jude tried to assimilate the scene below. Two people were lying facedown on the ground. Chase stood over them with a gun—*a gun*—in his hand.

In horror, Jude's hand went to her mouth. "No," she whispered. "Don't do this, Chase. Whatever it is, don't do it."

But he *was* doing it. She watched, wild-eyed, while he put handcuffs on the two people, securing their hands behind their backs, and stared while he poked through two bags on the ground next to them. One of the men on the ground started yelling, and Chase yelled something back.

Frightened out of her wits, Jude stood there, frozen in place. Chase yanked the two people to their feet and began pushing them away from the landing strip and toward the hill.

Panicked, Jude teetered between running and staying. She hesitated a tad too long, because Chase suddenly saw her. "Jude!"

She began to weep, hysterically, and turned and ran down the hill. It seemed to take an eternity to reach her car, but she finally did it, crying and gasping for air. She scrambled behind the wheel and started the motor with a roar.

Turning the car around as fast as she could, she sped away, nearly blinded by tears. Finally realizing that there was no longer a reason to drive without headlights, she switched them on and continued her reckless flight. There was no phone at the ranch. She should call the police—not *should*—she amended on a wrenching sob, *had to*.

She would drive to Sam Shelton's place. What else could she do? Chase was involved in something terrible, *doing* something terrible, and she couldn't stand by and pretend not to have witnessed it.

The car suddenly hit a bad hole and became airborne. In the next instant it came down with a bone-jarring crash and stopped dead. Shaken up and stunned, Jude struggled to get her bearings. She had to escape. Frantically she tried to restart the engine. It turned over but wouldn't start.

Jude dashed the tears from her eyes with a trembling hand and tried the motor again. "Start," she cried, and looked behind her through the back window of the car.

There were lights some distance back; Chase's headlights. She turned the ignition key again and heard only a grinding noise. "Start, please start," she moaned. For a moment she gave up and put her head on the steering wheel.

But then, after one last unsuccessful attempt to start the car, she jumped out of it and started running, cutting across the pasture in a more direct route to the compound.

Spotting Jude's car in the road, Chase stopped his truck and got out. The two drug dealers were handcuffed to the bed of the truck and temporarily out of commission, so he was a lot more worried about Jude than he was about those two lowlifes.

He approached Jude's car. "Jude?" A peek inside evidenced her absence. Scowling, worried that she was scared out of her mind and apt to do anything, he yelled, "Jude!

Answer me. I know you're out there and couldn't have gotten far. Jude!"

She put her hands over her ears and kept going, although her lungs felt close to bursting.

"Jude! I can explain everything. Listen to me. I'm a cop. Can you hear me? I'm a cop, Jude!"

Gasping and running, Jude heard only his voice. She finally reached the back of the barn and collapsed against it to catch her breath. Shorty ran up and yapped. Jude looked down at him and felt the tears starting again.

In the distance she saw the headlights of Chase's pickup moving again, getting closer. It struck her that hiding anywhere in the compound was a foolish idea. He would find her.

She lit out again for open country, and Shorty followed. "Go back, Shorty!" But Shorty stayed right behind her. Stumbling into a ditch, Jude huddled down and Shorty leapt into the ditch beside her. "Shorty, you idiot," she whispered raggedly, hugging the little dog to her chest.

He happily lapped her cheek and snuggled down on her lap.

Jude cautiously peeked over the edge of the ditch. The compound was a long way off, but she could see Chase's pickup parked near the house. There was a light on in the kitchen, so he was in the house looking for her.

Her heart was beating so hard she could hear it. "Quiet, Shorty," she whispered when he whimpered.

Chase came outside and yelled, "Jude!"

She slid below the edge of the ditch and closed her eyes, positive that she was escaping something horrible.

"Shorty!" was Chase's next shout.

Neither Jude nor Shorty appeared. Chase looked at his truck. He had to get those two scumbags booked and in jail where they belonged.

He went back inside, found a piece of paper and a pen and wrote a note, which he left on the kitchen table.

Then he slammed through the back door and strode to his pickup.

The sound of it leaving brought Jude's head up again. She watched until the taillights disappeared and even then wasn't sure she should leave the safety of the ditch.

After a good long while, she rubbed Shorty's ears. "Looks like you've been deserted, pal. Thunder, too. That's some great master you've got."

Exhausted and moving slowly, Jude made her way through the dark pasture to the compound. She passed the barn and the bunkhouse, every building gleaming with new paint, and finally entered the house.

The kitchen light had been left on. Not knowing whether she should start walking to Sam Shelton's place or what, she got a drink of water and then stood there in a daze.

Her gaze fell on the table . . . and the piece of paper on it.

With very little enthusiasm, or even curiosity, she walked over to the table and picked up the paper. It took about two seconds to see that Chase had left her some kind of message.

Sitting down wearily, Jude read it.

Jude,

I know you're scared right now, and when you get over that, you'll start hating me. But before you pass final judgment, give me a chance to explain in person. I'm a cop, Jude, and the two people I arrested tonight are drug smugglers. They've been using the ranch to fly heroin into Nevada, and I came out here to nail them.

Please take care of Shorty and Thunder until I can get back. It shouldn't be more than a day or two.

Chase

Bewildered, Jude read it again. He was a cop? It wouldn't quite sink in. Why had he kept his true identity from *her?*

The horrible fear she had suffered during the last horrible hour came rushing in on her with the impact of a tornado. She began trembling and couldn't control it. A cop, and he had put her through that? What kind of man was he?

Eleven

Jude was dragged out of a deep sleep the next morning by the slamming of a car door. Groggily she got out of bed and went to the window. Below were two cars. A uniformed police officer was walking toward the back door of the house.

Grabbing her robe, Jude hurried from her room and down the stairs. The officer was knocking on the door for the second time when she opened it.

"Miss Colter?"

Jude was tying the sash of her robe. "Yes, I'm Judith Colter."

"I have a court order which allows us to proceed onto your land to..."

"It's not necessary. Do whatever you have to. Do you need to come into the house?"

"No, ma'am."

"Thank you." Wearily Jude closed the door. From the kitchen window she watched the officer return to his car and then both vehicles drove away. Obviously the officers had been informed of the ranch's layout, because the cars headed unerringly for the back road that would lead to the landing strip.

Jude didn't want to even think about Chase. Every time she did, her nose got stuffy from tears. But with relentless constancy his image intruded. The most disturbing question of the dozens bombarding her senses was, why hadn't he approached her as a police officer with a necessary investigation on her land? Why so much pretense for her benefit?

And then, standing at the kitchen window, her hair bedraggled from rolling and tossing, her eyes swollen from crying, the answer struck her. He'd thought she was involved!

She felt so incredibly foolish, so ridiculously dense, she wanted to die. While he'd been teasing her about Shorty, and grinning that cute grin of his, and making her fall for him because what else was she but a stupid woman with an easily turned head, he had been watching and suspecting her of smuggling drugs.

The inequity of their relationship was staggering. All along, tossing *ain'ts* and good-old-country-boy charm around by the bushel basketful, acting like he had no plans at all for his future and didn't give a damn about tomorrow, he'd been trying to catch her in a lie, a misstep. His questions came rushing back to taunt and hurt. *What do you think of that landing strip, Jude? What do you think that light is, Jude? What about your financial situation, Jude?*

And fool that she was, she had seen herself as falling in love. As starry-eyed, because his smile reached her soul and his touch brought life and excitement to her body. She had ignored her own standards of acceptable behavior with the opposite sex for him, and buried her misgivings over his lack of ambition. To be fair, he hadn't encouraged such a complete loss of self as she had undergone, but remembering how flagrantly she had pursued him *without* encouragement only made her feel worse.

The bottom line was that he had deceived her as callously as any man could do with a woman, and she would never forgive him. Never!

He had to come back. Thunder was in the corral and Shorty was here. Besides, Chase had clearly stated his intention to return in his note.

She thought of bolting, of being gone when he returned, and for a moment relished the image of him arriving and realizing that he would never have the chance to explain. Explain, ha! What kind of simpering story would he come up with to explain making love to her?

Jude bit her lip. He could be cruel about that if he wanted. He could tell her that she'd been easy, which was only the awful truth. He could say, "You were available and willing, so don't blame me now for any regrets you're feeling."

Choking on a wounded sob, Jude rubbed her aching temples. She couldn't desert Thunder and Shorty. What if Chase didn't come for them right away? Besides, she had to finish painting the interior of the house. Selling the ranch was crucial.

Dispiritedly, Jude left the window and put on a pot of coffee. Just because she felt like the sun had dropped out of the sky didn't mean that life didn't go on. Her life, as dismal as it looked right now, consisted of finishing her work on the ranch and then hightailing it for a city with accounting firms and jobs.

Only one certainty had lodged in Jude's brain with that progression of thoughts: she would *not* be moving to Reno.

Seated in Captain Ryder's office, Chase waited while the senior officer read his report on last night's arrests.

The captain lifted his eyes from the papers. "Well, you were right."

"Moreno was right. What's going to happen to him now?"

Ryder removed his reading glasses and lay them on the desk. "We'll keep our part of the bargain. He'll be charged with a lesser crime than he would have been."

Chase said grimly, "And he'll be back on the streets within the year."

"Probably," Ryder agreed.

"Those two I nabbed last night should each get twenty years."

"It was a major bust, Chase. Besides putting one pipeline into Nevada out of commission."

The captain tapped the report in front him. "There's no mention of that Colter fellow in this."

Chase rubbed his mouth. "Uh, first, Colter isn't a fellow. He's a she and her name is Jude—Judith. She wasn't involved, Captain. I had to be sure, and she never caught on to my cover, but last night proved that she knew nothing about the scheme."

"You're positive? Seems mighty strange that she wouldn't know a plane was landing on her ranch."

"She hadn't lived there very long." Chase detailed Jude's background and reason for moving to Nevada, noting that Captain Ryder ultimately seemed satisfied that Jude had been no more than an innocent bystander in the nefarious scheme.

A little self-conscious then, Chase fanned his hand and looked at his fingernails. "Guess you should know, Captain." His eyes lifted. "I'm interested in Jude on a personal level."

"Oh? Well, thanks for telling me, but your personal life's your own, Chase. If it's serious, good luck." He stood and offered his hand. After the handshake, Chase left.

He was dead on his feet. After bringing in the two men he had arrested, he'd spent hours on paperwork. All he could think about was heading home and crashing. But there was one more task that needed doing before he could sleep.

On his way through the building, he stopped in at his own department, said a few words to the officers he encountered, and checked the duty roster. The line with his name contained only blank spaces because of his prolonged absence, which was the way he wanted it for another week. With a pen he wrote On Vacation next to his name and extended the information through the spaces for the next seven days.

Satisfied then, Chase headed for home and bed.

Jude opened the bunkhouse door and peered in. Chase's unmade bed caught her eye, then his clothes hanging on the wall hooks. Leaving the door ajar, she went inside.

Her heart was beating erratically, but she wasn't in there to snoop. Angrily she scooped the bedding off the bed and tossed it into a pile on the floor. She whipped into the bathroom and gathered up every towel and washcloth, both soiled and unused, returning to the main room to add them to the bedding.

What else?

There was nothing else, she decided. Everything else in the bunkhouse, other than a few bathroom supplies, belonged to Chase. Letting her gaze sweep the room, she spotted a few magazines on the nightstand, a canvas clothes bag in a corner, obviously containing his dirty jeans, and some fresh jeans and shirts on hangers on the wall hooks. A pair of boots sat next to his old suitcase and the boxes he'd used to bring his things to the ranch.

Jude didn't have to wonder to know that there wouldn't be one scrap of real information about Chase in the bunkhouse. He was a good cop, apparently, willing to do anything to stop a criminal, and he wasn't apt to leave anything lying around that would give away his cover. That was well and good. Jude respected the law and those who dedicated their lives to administering it.

But Chase had hurt her on a whole different level, and whether her resentment was completely rational or not, it was an abiding part of her.

She wanted to eradicate every trace of him from the ranch; the best she could do at the moment was to launder and put away the bedding and towels he had used.

Gathering them into a bundle, Jude picked it up and carried it outside. She stopped to close the door before hauling the load to the house.

That afternoon, with the washer and dryer running and Jude up to her eyeballs in white paint in the living room, someone knocked on the kitchen door. Gritting her teeth in case it was Chase, Jude went to answer.

It was the same officer who had awakened her that morning. "Yes?" she asked coolly.

"We brought your car, Miss Colter."

"My car?" Jude's eyes widened when she saw her car next to the officer's. "Oh." Her anger deflated. "How...? I mean, it wouldn't start."

"It was only a loose battery cable, ma'am. Sutton requested that one of us take a look at it. It's all fixed and ready to go."

"Thank you," Jude said quietly. "I really appreciate it."

The officer smiled. "There'll be a couple of trucks coming along, ma'am. To pick up the plane and car at the landing strip. By tonight everything will be removed from your property. Two officers will remain on duty until then."

Jude nodded. "Thanks, I appreciate the information."

The officer tipped his hat and walked away. Unsettled again, Jude closed the door.

Chase slept the day away and awoke after dark ravenously hungry. There was nothing in the house to eat, so he dressed and went out for a meal. He ordered a steak and a baked potato with butter and sour cream and thought about Jude while he ate it. He remembered her determination to serve wholesome meals and chuckled slightly, recalling her comments about him losing his good health if he continued to eat animal fat. He took another bite of steak and sighed happily.

But he wasn't at all happy, not in a way it counted. He wouldn't rest completely easy again until he'd made peace with Jude. And maybe made some time with her, as well. He couldn't think of her without also thinking of making love, and he was wondering, as Captain Ryder had, if what he felt for Jude was serious.

One thing was certain. What he felt for Jude Colter was more serious than any yen he'd ever before had for a woman. Not being completely cognizant on the subject of marriage, picket fences and babies, as those were subjects he had rather diligently avoided in the past, Chase couldn't predict where he and Jude might end up, even with a ''go'' from her. And there was every chance of that particular word never passing her lips where he was concerned.

He would return to the ranch in the morning. There wasn't much doubt in his mind that Jude would let him know how she felt the minute she saw him. Hoping that she would allow him to explain was all he could do at this point.

Jude heard a vehicle approaching and knew instinctively who was coming. Tearing the scarf from her head and flipping her hair around to loosen it, she ran to a mirror. It had been an involuntary reaction, and the instant she looked at herself, her lips tensed. What did it matter how she appeared to Chase? Damn him!

He didn't immediately knock on the door. After a few nerve-shattering minutes of waiting, Jude went to the kitchen window. Chase was bending over and petting an extremely delighted Shorty. Jude's heart nearly stopped. She had been bolstering hatred for Chase, deliberately feeding it with pain-filled memories, and all it took to make her feel like bawling again was one look at him.

Some stubborn part of herself would never hate Chase, no matter what he had done in the past or what he might do in the future. It was an eye-opening moment for Jude. When she left the ranch, Nevada, and Chase Sutton, she would be leaving behind a critical section of her soul.

Weakly she pressed her forehead against the cabinet at the side of the window. She had intended giving Chase what-for with both barrels, and certainly she couldn't act as if nothing had happened.

But neither could she start screeching the second she saw him.

Taking another look out the window, Jude saw him sauntering—the wretch was actually *sauntering*—down to the corral. His loose-gaited, untroubled stride made her see red, and for a minute she reconsidered her decision against screeching. He stroked Thunder's nose and fed him something, a carrot maybe, or an apple.

And finally, at long last, he glanced at the house. Jude jumped back from the window with her heart in her throat. If he dared, *dared,* to act as though she shouldn't be angry or upset, she would brain him!

Jude opened the door with an ice-cold expression and stepped outside. She waited for Chase to come closer and didn't make his stroll from the corral any easier for him by deflecting her harsh stare.

He saw her waiting, and swallowed the nervous lump in his throat. The gap between them closed, until he was standing only a few feet away.

"Hello, Jude."

She nodded, once.

"Uh, you read my note, I expect."

"I read it."

"I owe you an apology. Will you listen to it?"

She looked away for a moment, then back to him. "If it's brief. I'm busy."

"I came out here to check on a story I got from a street pusher. He said that heroin was being flown into Nevada via the Colter Ranch. Everyone I talked to about this place was positive no one had lived on it for years, so when I saw your sign advertising for a handyman, I couldn't figure out what Jude Colter was doing out here. Anyway, it seemed like—"

Jude interrupted. "This is not brief, Chase."

"Jude, please. You have to know everything."

She remained forbidding. "Why?"

"Because . . ." Chase took a breath. "Because something happened with you and me, and we can't just drop it."

"Oh, I think we can. In fact, consider it already dropped. I do."

"Jude, I don't believe that." This was worse than the tongue-lashing he'd envisioned receiving from her. She was so cold, so firmly set against him. His voice became gentler. "Don't be mad at me, Jude. I was only doing my job."

"Your handyman's job? I don't recall that your required duties included having sex with the boss, do you?"

"That's not fair, Jude. I did nothing you didn't want."

Her eyes began blazing. "Don't beat around the bush, Chase. Say it right out. *I* made the first pass!"

He clamped his lips together and looked away from her angry face. "I didn't come here to trade insults with you."

"No, you came for your animals. Get them, Chase, and get out of my sight. I never want to set eyes on you again." Jude rushed into the house and slammed the door. Then, literally too weak to remain standing, she slumped onto a kitchen chair. That wasn't what she had wanted to say at all. He would leave—what man wouldn't?—and she would never see him again.

Holding herself, Jude rocked back and forth, moaning in misery. She had handled the situation stupidly, letting her anger get the better of her tongue. Regret brought tears to her eyes and, once unleashed, they kept coming.

And then she remembered the wages she owed Chase. His unpaid salary suddenly seemed like a lifeline. He had earned the money, regardless of the rotten trick he'd been playing on her. Jumping up, Jude ran through the house and upstairs to get her money box. Quickly she computed the days Chase had worked times twenty and counted out the correct amount of cash.

She stopped in the bathroom to bathe her red eyes with cool water, but didn't dawdle. It wouldn't take him long to hitch up the horse trailer and load Thunder. His things in the bunkhouse would take only a few minutes to gather up and carry out to his truck.

Calmer through intense effort, Jude returned to the first floor and went outside. Her startled gaze found Chase sitting in a shiny, blue, late-model pickup with the door hanging open. He hadn't even *started* hitching up the horse trailer.

He saw her coming and slowly got out. This time it was him watching *her* walking closer, and a muscle in his jaw jumped from tension because he honestly didn't know what to expect now.

She held out her hand. "Here are the wages I owe you."

Chase stared at the cash. "I don't want your money."

"Well, you're going to take it!" Jude yelled.

"Like hell I am!" Chase yelled back. "There's only one thing I want from you and that's a few minutes of reasonably normal conversation. Consider *that* my wage, okay?"

"I hate you!"

"You do not!"

They stood there glaring at each other, almost toe-to-toe, neither backing down an inch.

Jude lifted her chin. "What makes you so smugly certain that I don't hate you?"

"I just know." Chase looked off for a few seconds, then back to her. "Jude, I don't play around on the job. What happened between us was way out of line. I thought about it right away, make no mistake, but I fought it every step of the way. That's why I concocted that story about falling off a horse and hurting my back."

"You thought I was involved in smuggling drugs," Jude accused, a bitter twist to her mouth. "And even then, believing those awful things about me, you...you..."

"I made love to you."

"Yes, damn you."

"And you made love to me. Are you damning yourself, too?"

"I thought you were an ordinary person."

"You thought I was a drifter, Jude, a man without roots. Don't gloss it over at this point. My lack of assets and ambition worried you. You didn't want to fall for a guy with nothing but a teasing grin, and you were doing it, anyway, which scared the holy hell out of you. Do you think I didn't know what was going on behind the questions you asked, and the hints about my shoddy equipment, my pointless lifestyle?"

"You treated me like a common criminal," Jude said sullenly.

"I treated you like a woman who I was *afraid* might be mixed up in something criminal," Chase rebutted. "And I also treated you like a woman I respected and wanted. Jude..." He took a small step forward and tried to touch her.

She jumped back as though burned. "Don't you dare!"

Chase dropped his hands. "Fine, I won't touch you. But there's still something I have to clear up on this ranch."

"Haven't you *cleared up* enough?" she said sarcastically.

"It's about money."

Frowning, Jude brought the cash up again. "Take it. You earned it."

"If you offer me that money again, I swear I'll set a match to it," Chase said furiously.

"Then what money are you talking about?"

"The money in the toolshed."

Everything in Jude went still, her anger, her resentment, her own personal battle because she didn't want to fight with Chase and couldn't seem to stop herself.

"In *my* toolshed?" she echoed in disbelief. Her head turned so she could see the building. "In *that* toolshed?"

She didn't know about it. Chase released a long breath. "There's a canvas bag filled with cash under a pile of junk in there, Jude. I found it the day I went looking for the wire stretcher."

Her head jerked around. "What did you think, that I was hiding cash to pay for drugs?"

"It crossed my mind, yes," Chase said evenly.

"I've never broken the law in my life, and if I was so inclined," Jude said low and passionately, "it wouldn't be with drugs. I despise drug pushers and smugglers."

"So do I, Jude. It's the reason I'm working narcotics."

Their gazes collided and held through several tense moments. His blue eyes rivaled the sky for depth and color, only she had never seen a sky with such life and emotion as she was looking at this second. This man, intense, intelligent and dedicated, was the person she'd caught glimpses of in the laid-back persona of drifter he'd introduced to her.

She looked away first. "Show me that money."

Chase nodded and started walking. He stopped when Jude didn't move. "Come on. I'd like you to see how it's concealed. I put everything back the way I found it."

Jude went, but she made sure there was distance between them while they walked. She hadn't forgiven him, but her anger was shrinking. Whether that was because she was beginning to grasp his side of this fiasco or because she was simply too far gone on him to stay angry for long, Jude didn't know. Unquestionably his goal in the whole mess hadn't been to deliberately hurt her, even if that was what had happened.

But he had also let her know that he'd wanted her right from the first, and that one fact had wormed its way into her brain and emotions with the tenacity of a bulldog.

At the toolshed, Chase pushed open the door and waited for Jude to precede him through it. She brushed past him quickly, all too aware of his scent and warmth as she passed.

"It's over there," Chase said, and moved her aside by taking hold of her shoulders.

Jude gasped. "Don't!"

"I only needed to get past you. There's very little walking space in here, Jude."

"Just don't take advantage of every opportunity," she demanded sharply.

"Wouldn't dream of it." Chase pointed to a pile of junk. "It's at the bottom of that."

Jude studied the pile, then glanced around the smelly little shed. "I probably never would have cleaned this out. It would take a semi to haul it all off."

"Like you said, Simon Colter rarely threw anything away." Chase began shoving junk around. After a few minutes he came up with a canvas bag. "This is it. Ever see it before?"

Jude's eyes sparked dangerously. "If you ask me one more *cop* question, I'll never speak to you again."

"Jude, I'm merely asking if you saw this bag before. In the family, maybe."

"I told you I was taken from this place at five years of age. I never saw that bag before, nor one like it. It sort of resembles a briefcase, though."

"Or a book bag. It reminds me of the kind of book bags students used before they started carrying backpacks."

Jude nodded. "You're right. I've seen them in movies."

Chase grinned, the first Jude had seen today. "Want to see the money?"

"Well, it's not mine. Why would I care?" Jude scoffed.

Chase's grin got wider. "It might be yours."

"Yeah, right."

"Jude, who else's would it be? Assuming it's not counterfeit or identified as involved in a criminal action, that is."

"Identified?"

"By individual bill number or some sort of marking. In cases of cash exchanged for kidnap victims, for example, the bills are often marked in such a way as to be pretty much invisible to the naked eye. A lab test is all it takes, though."

Jude eyed the bag with more interest. "Are you saying the cash in that bag might belong to me?"

"Don't get your hopes too high, but it is possible. Look, I've gone around in circles on this money. Those drug smugglers I arrested never once came near the compound, so it didn't belong to them. They talked a mile a minute once they realized what deep sh—" Chase cleared his throat "—uh, trouble they were in."

"How much money is there?"

"Lots. Want to count it?"

"Do we dare? What if it is marked? Wouldn't handling it destroy the marks?"

"Nope. Nothing can destroy the marks, short of burning it. Which, I might add, had me worried. This place would burn to the ground in five minutes."

"But who put it there?"

Chase cocked an eyebrow. "Uncle Simon?"

Jude laughed, albeit grimly. "I doubt that. I don't think Uncle Simon ever had an extra nickel. I went through a dozen boxes of his old papers and junk, and there wasn't even one bank statement."

Her mouth dropped open. Chase threw back his head and laughed. "That could be the answer, Jude. Maybe Uncle Simon preferred this canvas bag over banks."

Twelve

"**W**ould you like to come in?" Jude asked with a nod of her head at the house.

Chase could see in her eyes that all had not been forgiven or forgotten, but at least the yelling had stopped.

"Thanks," he said quietly.

Jude led the way and didn't even try to make small talk. "You can sit at the kitchen table to count the money," she said when they were inside. "I'm going to take a shower."

Chase raised an eyebrow. "You don't want to stay here while I count it?"

"No. In the first place, I doubt if it's mine. In the second, if you intended helping yourself, you would already have done so."

"A logical woman," he remarked with a laugh.

Jude made a quick exit and darted up the stairs. Chase being in the house, when only a short time ago she'd been thinking about him and mayhem in the same breath, wasn't exactly a comfortable situation. But down deep, where it mattered, she was glad that he hadn't gone off in a huff because of her nasty attitude.

Inside she was still at war, she realized, when her defense mechanism kicked in because of that "nasty attitude" business. Who had a better right to attitude at the present? She had been stomped on, kicked in the teeth and run over by a steamroller. Or, at least, her emotions felt bruised enough to have suffered such a devastating onslaught.

At any rate, a little time alone seemed necessary to her mental health. Chase's grin was already getting adorable, and they had only stopped hurling insults at each other a few minutes ago.

Sighing, Jude entered the shower stall and turned her face up to the spray.

Downstairs, Chase lay out the cash in neat rows on the table. When the canvas bag was empty, he got up and put on a pot of coffee, realizing that he felt freer in Jude's kitchen today than he ever had in disguise. Probably because he was only one person today—himself.

He took a stroll through the first floor rooms and saw that the living room walls had a new coat of paint. Spying a drying pan of paint and a crusty roller, he carried them outside to the yard spigot and ran water over the tools.

Rubbing his mouth thoughtfully, he glanced around. He really liked this place. But how did Jude feel about it? For that matter, how did Jude feel about him? Chase amended the thought again. How did Jude feel about him *now?* Not too many days ago he'd had a pretty good idea of what was going on in her mind, but now?

Returning to the house, Chase poured himself a cup of coffee. He was sitting at the table again when Jude came in. She was wearing clean jeans and shirt, and her wet hair was smoothed back from her face.

Chase watched her gaze go to the money. "It adds up to twenty-six thousand, five hundred dollars," he announced.

"That's quite a sum."

"Yes, it is."

Jude spotted the pot of fresh coffee and went to the cabinet for a cup. "So, what do you do now?"

"Take it to the lab for examination. I'll sign it in under your name. If there's no record of the bill numbers, and no concealed marks, it's yours."

"I could use it," Jude said dryly.

"I thought at first it might be that windfall you mentioned."

She rolled her eyes. "That was a lie. I don't have any money coming in."

"Why did you lie about it, Jude? That was one of the reasons I kept worrying that you might be involved with the drug shipment."

Jude stood at the window with her back to the room. She brought the cup of coffee to her lips for a sip. "I've never liked talking about money, particularly with someone I'd just met. I don't know. It was a stupid lie, but it just came rolling out."

She turned to see Chase. "You don't look like any cop I ever knew."

He grinned sheepishly, because that was almost precisely the comment he'd made about her accounting career.

Jude sighed. "But then, you don't look like a down-on-your-luck cowboy, either. Guess I was an easy target."

Chase slowly stood. "Don't keep throwing that word around. I already told you I never thought of you as easy."

She looked down into her cup. "Sorry, but the shoe fits so well I keep forgetting."

"What do you want me to say, Jude? I'm sorrier than I can tell you. I felt like sh—like *dirt* after— Aw, hell, I don't know *what* to say."

"You scared me out of ten years' growth the other night."

"I know I did."

"I saw you with that gun, and those two people on the ground." Jude's empty hand went to her throat. "I . . . was worried all along that you might be hiding out here from the law, and . . . Damn it, Chase, don't laugh. It's not funny."

He erased the laughter from his expression. "I know it's not. Jude, I've got a week off."

Startled, her eyes darted to his. "Meaning?"

"I want to finish the fence repairs."

She stared. "You're not serious."

"It's important to me, Jude. I want to finish what I started here."

For some crazy reason she suspected he wasn't only talking about the fence. Her face colored. "Uh, that's not a good idea, Chase."

"Are you afraid of what might happen between us if we spend another week together?" he asked softly.

"No, I am not," she denied sharply. "But it's just not a good idea."

"I'd stay in the bunkhouse."

"Well, of course you'd stay in the bunkhouse. But you're not *going* to stay in the bunkhouse." Jude set her cup on the counter to massage her temples. "You're confusing me."

Chase came around the table but didn't advance so far that Jude would feel pressured. "By your own admission, you're short of money. Jude, I'm offering the sweat of my brow for free."

"That argument will get you nowhere," she scoffed.

"All right, what about this one? You need to get this place in shape to sell. How about if I volunteer a week of my time to atone for all the trouble I caused you. In return, to make you feel better about accepting my offer, you can pay me when you either sell the ranch or get possession of that cash on the table."

"Um, let me think for a minute, okay?"

"Sure, take your time." Chase went back to the table for his coffee cup, which he brought to the counter for a refill.

Jude moved politely out of his way, although he suspected the gesture was really to maintain some distance between them.

He could feel her deep inside of himself, even at a distance. Her face was shiny from her shower, and he liked that she hadn't put on makeup, although he suspected that, too, was for the benefit of distance, a psychological distance.

If that had been her intent, it wasn't working. She didn't need gunk on her face to be beautiful, nor perfume on her body to be sexy. Jude was just naturally beautiful and sexy. She couldn't alter those traits, any more than she could help being female.

She was also naturally amiable, and he knew from experience that she couldn't stay angry for long. Give them a few days together and they'd be laughing as though nothing had happened.

"What d'ya say?" he finally asked teasingly when she seemed to be getting nowhere with a decision.

But she didn't smile in response as he'd hoped. "Would you agree to a few ground rules?"

"I don't see why not," Chase replied.

Jude studied him searchingly and then looked away. She had slipped badly with Chase and had no intention of repeating herself. His apologies felt strangely akin to an insult, as though he was remembering how uninhibitedly she'd behaved and was hoping to pick up where they'd left off.

Still, something urgent and pressuring within her wouldn't permit a scathing denial of further involvement. It wasn't clear in her mind what she hoped to gain from the arrangement he offered, other than solid fencing on the ranch, but she still wasn't ready for a permanent and final break with Chase.

She returned an unflinching gaze to his face. "No foolishness, Chase. Nothing personal between us. You take care of the fencing and leave it at that."

He couldn't prevent a hint of a grin. "Agreed."

"And please don't think I'm not serious."

"It would never cross my mind," he said solemnly. Chase went to the money and began scooping it into the canvas bag. "I'll take this to Reno to the lab right now. I'll be back tonight." He looked up. "Why don't you come along? We could have dinner in Reno."

The invitation startled Jude. "Uh, no, but thanks for asking."

"Jude, you've been working hard for weeks. Dinner in a nice restaurant would do you a world of good."

And what would it do for you? There was still too much resentment in Jude's system to kiss and make up, which she was honest enough to recognize and face for what it was. The plain truth was that she would rather be alone for the rest of today than struggle through an unknown number of hours in Chase's company. Without question, the wounds from his deceit were not going to easily vanish.

"Maybe another time." She spoke without rancor but with firmness, and Chase got the message and finally accepted it.

"All right, another time," he said quietly. With the bag buckled shut, he carried it to the door. "I'll see you later."

"Fine."

But after he had driven away, Jude wondered if "fine" wasn't asking for another bout of heartache. Her ambivalence with Chase was disturbing. However noble his cause when barging into her life, he had run roughshod over her emotions. Perhaps he regretted it. Maybe his apologies contained sincerity. But at the end of one more week they would still be saying goodbye and going their separate ways.

And if she had any hope of something different in the back of her mind, she had better reexamine her priorities. Chase would make love to her again...this time without any of the reluctance he'd apparently felt when he'd been on duty and she had been a suspect.

But she was long past the fling-for-a-night stage with Chase. The past few days had matured her enormously. The next time she gave so willingly to a man, she would be seeking commitment. That was a personal ground rule just recently devised, but it was one Jude fully intended to live by.

Chase got back to the ranch after dark that night. There were no lights on in the main house, indicating to him that Jude had already retired. Shorty wriggled his way into the bunkhouse with him, and Chase snapped on a light. His bed was neatly made, and when he drew back the blankets he saw clean sheets. In the bathroom, clean towels and washcloths were laid out.

But his biggest surprise was the array of freshly laundered clothing on the wall hooks. His laundry bag was empty, and all of the dirty jeans and shirts it had contained had been washed, dried, neatly placed on hangers and hung on the hooks.

For some reason Jude's simple act of kindness touched Chase in a profound way. Jude Colter was blessed with a streak of just plain goodness, which Chase, in his line of work, didn't run into everyday. When he did meet people who believed that basic decency was only the norm and lived their lives accordingly, he invariably liked them.

He liked Jude. The Jude Colters of the world were those women who became loyal, loving wives and mothers. They were the women attending PTA meetings, and heading Scout troops, and teaching Bible classes to the youngsters of their church.

They were the sort of gal who would wash a man's dirty clothes when she had damn good cause for clouting him alongside the head.

Chase went to bed vowing to make things easier for Jude. He would finish repairing those fences and clean out the toolshed, and take care of any other chore he came across.

It was only when he got sleepy and on the verge of unconsciousness that the image of Jude's long, gorgeous legs filtered through the mist.

He fell asleep smiling.

Chase took his place at the breakfast table. "Thanks for doing my laundry."

"You're welcome."

Conversation came to a halt until their oatmeal bowls were empty. Chase put down his spoon and grinned. "I'm starting to like oatmeal."

"Not enough to order it in a restaurant, I'll bet," Jude said dryly.

Chase laughed. "Well, maybe not." He sat back. "So, are you going to work in the house today, or would you like to help me with the fencing?"

Jude avoided a direct exchange with his blue, blue eyes. "I'm going to stick with the house until it's done. Shouldn't be more than another few days."

"I noticed the living room yesterday. Looking good, Jude." What was "looking good" was her. It wasn't possible, in fact, to look at Jude and not think about how he'd *really* like to spend the day.

"By the way, thanks for soaking the paint pan and roller. I'd forgotten about them."

Chase smiled. "Well, you had other things on your mind."

"So I did," Jude agreed coolly. "Were there any comments on the money when you delivered it to the lab?"

"Speculation, of course. We could have an answer in a few days, although if any doubt about its ownership pops up, it could take longer. You know, this isn't like finding money in a public place, Jude. Then there's a waiting period involved while all claims are considered. You're the only one entitled to a claim in this case."

"Well, like I said yesterday, I could use it. But I'm not going to count on getting it until I hear from the lab." Jude stood. "In the meantime, it's business as usual."

Chase gulped the last of his coffee and got to his feet. "Anything you want done before I start on the fencing?"

Jude looked at him. He seemed so utterly guileless now. For the first time she thought about how tough it would be to bury one's true nature beneath a layer of pretense for days on end. He had succeeded well enough that it had taken her some time to begin seeing through his disguise, and even then she had only come up with him having some deep-seated personal problem and not that he was someone else entirely.

But this man, the one she was looking at right now, with his beguiling grin, and his shower-damp hair, and the sexiest mouth any human being ever possessed, was the *real* Chase Sutton. The genuine article.

Jude's heart took a sudden leap. If anyone was hiding behind a layer of pretense now, it was her. Wouldn't she just love to toss every drop of anger and resentment in the trash this very minute and tell him about the longing she felt simply because he was standing in her kitchen? About the hope in her soul because he hadn't written her off? No one had ordered him back here. No one had forced him to give up a week of his free time to help her out. Everything he was doing now was because he was a sincerely nice guy.

Discombobulated, Jude mumbled something about him going ahead with the fences and ran from the room and up the stairs. Chase's eyes registered surprise, but he let her go, realizing that they were bound to have some unsettling and probably puzzling moments. With his hat firmly on his head, he left the house to begin the day's work.

Trembling, Jude sat on her bed. She loved him. She had fallen in love with Chase practically at first sight, and it was the permanent, till-death-do-us-part kind of love. Nothing short of him telling her to get lost with his own sexy mouth would squelch the feeling, and even then she would probably suffer for a very long time.

The question now was, what was she going to do about it?

Chase came into the house for supper and smelled something so tantalizing his mouth watered. Jude was at the stove, and she turned with a warm smile. "Hope you like pork chops and milk gravy."

He raised an eyebrow. "I *love* pork chops and milk gravy, but aren't they loaded with cholesterol?"

Jude laughed. "It's a treat."

You're the treat, Chase thought with a noticeable rising of his blood pressure. She was wearing something pink and gauzy, a dress that floated with her movements. Her hair was curled and lustrous around her face, and the expression in her beautiful brown eyes could only be described as inviting.

He was thrilled but stunned. It didn't seem possible that she would be over her anger this soon. He'd known it would happen, that she wouldn't be able to sustain outrage for very long, but while digging post holes and stringing wire today, he could not have visualized walking in to this tonight.

"Go ahead and sit down," Jude told him. "Everything's ready." She began carrying bowls of food to the table.

Chase took his seat. "Any particular reason for this treat?" he asked casually.

Jude passed him the bowl of mashed potatoes. "I just thought you needed a good meal."

Her idea of a good meal was vegetarian stew, so Chase couldn't quite believe that line of baloney. Something was going on with Jude, and he was going to enjoy it to the max. He heaped his plate with mashed potatoes and milk gravy, green beans cooked with bacon and onion, and crisp, browned pork chops, and then loaded his salad bowl with green salad topped with a rich, creamy dressing.

She was a damn good cook when she put aside the dilemma that every American was facing on a daily basis, Chase realized. To indulge or not to indulge? was the question driving everyone to salads with tasteless dressings, and to eating very little meat, and never, ever getting near, heaven forbid, gravy.

Chase wasn't ignorant of statistics or advice from health experts, but he'd given up smoking because it wasn't healthy, and he exercised when he hated it because it was. He maintained his weight within a six pound variable, and he didn't mind eating healthy most of the time.

But there was a satisfaction to sitting down to a meal like this that was absent from nearly every other human pastime. Other than sex, of course. If a man had good food and good sex in his life—and work he enjoyed—he had very little to complain about.

Savoring a bite, Chase eyed the woman across the table. All three requirements for an uncomplaining life-style were sitting right at this table with him. Or, at least, were well within reach on Jude's land.

But was he ready to change his present life-style to attain it?

And there were no guarantees that Jude would agree. He had hurt her badly. A proposal of marriage from him would probably knock the socks she usually wore right off her feet. Tonight, he had noticed, she was wearing pretty slippers *without* socks.

"This is the best meal I've ever eaten," he declared.

"I think you said the same thing about that T-bone steak," Jude noted.

He looked at her and laughed. "Meant it, too. But this is really the best, Jude."

She liked watching him eat, although she was only picking at her own plate. "Chase..."

"Yeah?"

"I'd like to apologize for getting so worked up about what you did. You were only doing your job."

He lay down his fork. "I didn't like lying to you, Jude. Lying goes with undercover work. You can't slip into a situation and take on a different identity without lying. It never bothered me before, but it did with you."

"I don't like lies, either, and I wish I hadn't invented that stupid story about money coming in. It seems so foolish now."

"We all have our special points of pride, Jude."

"I suppose." She smiled, almost shyly. "There's chocolate cake with fudge frosting for dessert."

He grinned. "They always say the shortest route to a man's heart is through his stomach."

"Guess that's what I'm aiming for," Jude said softly.

Chase's grin faded while his pulse went crazy. His gaze locked with Jude's across the table, and he started to get up. Jude raised a hand. "Please. Finish your dinner first. There's no... hurry."

He licked his suddenly dry lips. "Maybe there is."

"I'm not going anywhere. I'll be here when you're through eating." Jude smiled. "I didn't cook this meal to see it thrown away because of a ... better idea."

"I've got a better idea, all right. And you know what it is, too, don't you?"

"Eat, Chase. Your food's getting cold."

The food was still good, delicious, in fact, but filling his stomach didn't seem nearly as important as it had a minute ago. Jude sitting there looking like the epitome of womankind and wearing a mysterious smile that made him think about the joys of sin, was a distraction he had one hell of a time ignoring.

But he cleaned his plate, all the while knowing that dessert wasn't going to be chocolate cake with fudge frosting. His gaze dropped to Jude's plate. "You didn't eat much."

"I nibbled while I was cooking."

"Guess nibbling is one of the hazards of cooking," he said softly. "Jude, may I get up now?"

"I wish you would," she said just as softly.

He rose slowly, moved around the table and held out his hand. Jude looked at it and then placed hers in it. He urged her up, and brought her into his arms with a sigh of supreme pleasure. "Do you forgive me, Jude?"

"You're forgiven," she whispered.

He leaned back to see her face. "What happened?"

Jude looked into his eyes. If he mentioned love right now she would confess hers. But there was an enormous risk to initiating the subject, and it was best to go slow at this point.

"I thought about the whole thing all day, Chase, and I just can't condemn you for being dedicated to your career."

He was watching her mouth, which he thought moved in the most exciting way imaginable when she spoke. It also moved, he recalled, in a very exciting way when she kissed.

"Maybe we should talk later," he suggested in a less steady voice.

Jude moved closer to him. "Maybe we should."

Chase's lips touched hers, at first gently and then with an explosive desire. A low moan built in Jude's throat as she kissed him back. They held each other as though permanently bonded, moving together as lovers do. Chase whispered while just barely lifting his mouth, "We've never made love on a bed, Jude."

"An easily rectified oversight," she whispered in return.

Arm in arm and starry-eyed, they deserted the kitchen and walked up the stairs to Jude's bedroom.

Thirteen

Chase was sleeping when Jude remembered the mess she had left in the kitchen. Knowing that if she ignored it now she would hate herself in the morning, she forced herself away from the warmth of Chase's body and silently slid off the bed. Clad in a robe, she padded downstairs barefoot.

It was even worse than she'd thought, she realized grimly while scanning the crusted pans and dishes. Fearing that any hesitation would send her scooting back up the stairs, she quickly ran hot water into the dishpan and added a generous squirt of liquid detergent.

In fifteen minutes the kitchen was back in good order. Satisfied, Jude dried her hands. Her gaze fell on the chocolate layer cake she had struggled to produce. Never had she made a cake from scratch before, but her supply of groceries had not included a cake mix. Luckily she had located a tattered but readable cookbook in one of the kitchen's many drawers.

She had eaten very little during dinner, and the cake suddenly looked extremely appetizing. Cutting herself a slice, Jude took the plate to the table. She was still enjoying her first bite when she heard from the second floor, "Jude? Are you down there?"

"I'm in the kitchen, Chase," she called. "Would you like some cake?"

"I'm not dressed."

Visualizing him at the head of the stairs stark naked, Jude smiled and called, "I'll bring some up." Quickly she cut another slice of cake and placed it on a dish. Carrying both plates and two forks, she snapped out the kitchen light with her elbow and trudged up the stairs.

Chase was sitting on the bed with the sheet over his lap. The lamp on the nightstand was on, so Jude was able to see the contented expression on his face very clearly. She smiled at him. "Here's your dessert."

"I already had dessert, sweetheart, but I don't mind seconds." His adorable grin positively melted Jude's insides.

She joined him on the bed, and they ate their cake with appropriate yummy sounds. "I want you to know this is a scratch cake," she told him with a mouthful.

"I knew that."

She socked him on the arm. "You did not!"

He smiled at her. "I can't tell if you're prettier at night or in the morning. 'Course, you're grouchier than a she-bear with cubs in the morning, and you're sweeter than sin at night."

"Speak for yourself, Sutton," she retorted.

They fell silent for a moment, then Chase said, "We get along, don't we?"

"Most of the time."

"What I mean is, we're a lot alike."

"Do you think so?"

"Both cranky in the morning, both hard workers, both sexy and good-looking."

"Don't forget shy and modest," Jude drawled dryly.

Chase grinned. "Facts are facts, sweetheart." He passed his empty plate to the nightstand and then watched her eat her last bite. "As good as that cake tastes, you taste better."

"As good as *I* taste," she returned without skipping a beat, *"you* taste better."

"Another common trait," Chase said solemnly. "We both taste better than homemade chocolate cake. There's just no end to our similarities."

Jude couldn't help laughing. "But I'm a cat person and you prefer dogs. What've you got to say about that?"

"That we're an almost perfect match," Chase said quietly.

He was no longer joking, Jude saw. She handed him her plate. "Please set that over there with yours."

With the dishes out of the way, Chase scooted down in the bed to lie on his side facing her, one arm crooked between his head and the pillow. Jude was sitting with her legs crossed in front of her, and her robe was draped to cover the essentials.

Deliberately, Chase moved a panel of the robe aside, exposing her charms to his gaze. Jude almost objected, but caught herself in time. Instead, pink-cheeked and with her thermostat working on high, she let him look his fill.

"You are seriously beautiful," he finally said huskily, hoisting himself up to an elbow so he could slide his hand up her inner thigh. It stopped precisely where she knew it would, and she suddenly couldn't breathe very well.

While caressing her intimately, he whispered, "Remember the day by the creek when I said I couldn't give you promises?"

"Yes," was all she could manage to whisper.

"It almost killed me to say that to you, but you understand now what I was getting at."

"I understand, yes. Chase..."

He bent forward and kissed her lips. "Do you like what I'm doing?"

She swallowed. "How about if I do it to you so you can find out for yourself?"

His grin flashed. "You've already done it and I already know I like it."

"You're a glib devil."

He kissed the corner of her mouth. "You're breathing hard, sweetheart."

"You're driving me crazy, *sweetheart.*"

"Then get out of that robe and under the covers." His grin was truly devilish this time. "Come and see what I've got for you."

"I can see what you've got from here," she retorted breathlessly.

But she shrugged the robe from her shoulders and began scooting under the covers. Chase opened his arms and then wrapped them around her. She snuggled against him and he immediately began caressing her breasts.

She closed her eyes to savor the warm, silky sensation. "Getting sleepy?" he teased.

Her lashes fluttered upward. "What do you think?"

"I think—" Chase paused to kiss her lips "—I'm in love with you."

Those lovely words, coming so suddenly, brought tears to Jude's eyes. "I didn't expect you to cry about it," he said in a teasing tone. But Jude also heard a note of apprehension and realized that he wasn't positive of her reaction.

She'd gone so many different ways with Chase, one time on, the next time off, that she wanted this to be perfect. He'd made mistakes in judgment with her, and certainly she hadn't been all that clearheaded with him. Taunting him into making love by taking off her clothes at the creek had been dirty pool, and she sure hadn't tried to stop him out by the corral a few nights later.

But then, she'd been in love all along, and his precarious situation hadn't permitted him to even consider such an attachment.

Chase was holding his breath. Obviously Jude's wheels were turning, and whatever came out of her mouth next was crucial.

She slid her forefinger up his chest, slowly, directing it to follow the curvature of his throat and jaw, and finally halting it on his mouth. "I've been in love with you since our first kiss. Possibly before that. That's what I finally accepted today, Chase. When you asked what happened to change my attitude, I told you I couldn't condemn you for doing your job. That's true, too. But I couldn't go on being angry and risking..." She looked him right in the eye and said flirtatiously, "You getting away from me."

He'd been listening rather dreamy-eyed, enchanted with her soft Texas drawl and the fact that she loved him, too. But when she said that she couldn't go on risking him getting away from her, he stiffened.

Jude stiffened, too. "I was only kidding, Chase," she said anxiously.

"You've been plotting marriage all along, haven't you?"

"Uh, I've thought... of it... a few times."

"Even when you believed I had no income or any plans to get an income, you set out to land me."

"I'm sorry," she said meekly. "Please don't..."

"You wanted me, and you used every trick in the book to reel me in."

"Just about," she admitted with guilt weakening her voice. "But I didn't consider what I was doing to be... trickery."

"No? What did you call it?"

Jude bit her lip. Her eyes were crinkled with worry. "I guess I called it love."

A slow smile tipped his lips. In the next instant he threw back his head and roared with laughter. Astonished, it took Jude a minute to realize he'd been teasing again.

"You...you..." she sputtered.

He took her flailing hands and held them. "I think you'd better finish what you started, don't you?" His eyes were dancing merrily.

"And just what do you mean by that?" she asked suspiciously.

"When a woman compromises a man's virtue, there's only one honorable conclusion, sweetheart."

"Are you suggesting that I propose to you?"

"Guess the ball's in your court," he said softly.

Jude blinked. There was still something teasing in his expression, but this wasn't all a big joke to Chase. Mingled with his laughter and impudence, and the sense of fun he portrayed, was a glimmer of uncertainty. It was that small peek into his psyche that touched Jude's soul. The confidence she had been lacking regarding Chase's feelings for her came rushing through her system like a speeding locomotive.

She drew a deep, slow breath. A marriage proposal had never crossed her lips. Until Chase, even her thoughts about marriage had been limited to "someday" and not particularly important.

But she was a completely different woman with Chase than she'd been with anyone else. And maybe he was a different man with her. Maybe he was as amazed to find himself in love and thinking about marriage as she was.

It was his way, she knew now, to tease and make jokes when he was nervous. That was the reason for all that nonsense about Shorty the day Chase arrived to ask about her handyman job. He hadn't expected Jude Colter to be a woman, and maybe he hadn't expected to feel something for her.

"I would love to propose to you," she purred.

Chase's eyes widened, immediately followed by a dazzling grin. He lay back on his pillow. "Shoot, sweetheart. I'm all ears."

"Are you really?" she said in her most seductive voice, and sat up.

Chase watched her. "Uh, what's on your mind?"

Unhurriedly she moistened her lips with the tip of her tongue. "Only a proper proposal, darling." Without haste, she pulled down the sheet, sliding it down, down, until Chase was uncovered to his knees. He helped then by kicking the sheet to the foot of the bed.

Leaning forward, Jude placed her lips into the curve of his throat and shoulder, where she nibbled delicately. "Ah, yes," she murmured. "No question about it. You taste *much* better than chocolate cake."

Chase chuckled. "That's because you want my bod."

"Don't ever doubt it," she whispered, bringing her mouth down to his chest. Slowly, deliberately, she kissed a path to his belly.

"Is this proper procedure for a marriage proposal?" Chase asked on a ragged breath.

Jude noticed that he was no longer chuckling. "Surely you didn't expect me to just blurt it out. Preliminaries are extremely important in this sort of thing."

"Your preliminaries are giving me some very big ideas, sweetheart."

"So I see," Jude said pertly. Her ensuing kisses and caresses had him digging his fingernails into the mattress. She raised up to look at his face. "Do I have your undivided attention, Mr. Sutton?"

"Undivided," Chase gasped.

Jude crawled up his body and lay on top of him. She took his face between her hands and pressed her mouth to his. Desire exploded between them. Chase's arms came up around her and, almost roughly, he rolled them over so he was on top.

His eyes were smoky and hot. "You were saying?" he whispered.

Jude tenderly touched his face. "You're so handsome you take my breath."

"That's not what you were saying," he rebutted, turning his head to nibble on her fingers.

Again a sense of fun had sparked between them. "I love you. Was that what I was saying?"

"I like hearing that and I love you, too, but there was something else."

"Um, could it be this? I love you madly and would like to bear your children."

"Close, but no cigar," Chase murmured while nuzzling her neck.

"Your preliminaries are marvelous," Jude breathed.

"The preliminaries are over, sweetheart," he growled. "Let's get to the main event. I've got one in mind that..."

"Will you marry me?" she whispered.

Everything changed. Chase looked at her with a melting expression. Jude looked at him with her heart in her eyes. For a few incredible moments they communicated without words, and if her entire past didn't flash through Jude's mind, the future certainly did.

"Will you marry me?" Chase said softly.

Jude smiled. "I asked you first, but my answer is yes."

"So is mine."

And then neither thought again of preliminaries. Joined in the most elemental way, Chase took Jude to the stars. She clung and moaned and lifted to meet the thrusts of his body, and at the final ecstasy, she wept.

But so did Chase. Jude kissed away the moisture beneath his eyes with soft avowals of eternal love, and then they turned out the light and curled up together.

The silence of the night seemed to contain a new and profound meaning for Jude. Snuggled within Chase's protective and loving embrace, she remembered the events that had brought them together, and rendered the wandering of her mind as the most pleasant of ways to fall asleep.

It surprised her to hear, "Jude?"

She smiled in the dark. "I thought you had fallen asleep."

"There's something I need to know."

"Ask me anything, Chase."

"How do you feel about the ranch?"

"*This* ranch?"

"Yes, this ranch. How do you feel about it?"

Jude had been lying with her back nestled into the inside curve of Chase's body. She turned to face him. "I don't really feel much of anything about it, Chase. It represents a good deal of money, which is important. I'm not sure I understand what you mean."

"Do you like it at all?"

"Like it? Uh, I guess so. Actually, I really do like this house. It's got oodles of room, and with a little modernizing and imagination, could be turned into something special. Why are you asking me these things?"

"Have you been lonely out here? Or afraid?"

Jude laughed. "I was getting a little lonely before you came along, but as for being afraid, fear never entered my mind until a certain handsome cop arrested a couple of bad guys one night."

Chase hugged her closer and planted a brief but passionate kiss on her lips. "You'll never be put in jeopardy again, I swear it."

"I'm not worried," Jude said dreamily. She paused to remember the topic. "Why are you asking about my feelings for the ranch?"

"Because I really like it."

Jude frowned. "But... you're a cop. You have a job, a career. You couldn't live here and work in Reno."

"No, I couldn't."

"You've been thinking about... living here," she said slowly. "Do you know anything about raising cattle?"

"A little. I've got a few friends in the business."

"You realize that I know nothing about it."

"What I realize, Jude, is that you've got more spunk than any woman I've ever known. More than most men. How many people do you know that would take on the job you did here? Not very many, I'll bet."

"It didn't seem like I had a choice," Jude replied.

"Aren't you the one who told me we always have choices?"

Jude was silent a moment. "Guess we're looking at one right now."

"Only if you agree to think about it. If you know right now that you don't like the idea, that'll be the end of it."

"And we would live in Reno?"

"Reno's my home, honey. I have a pretty decent house in a good residential area. I think you'll like it."

He wasn't going to try to talk her into a decision favoring the ranch, Jude realized. "I'll think about it," she said quietly.

Chase hugged her. "Thanks."

Think about it she did. Long after Chase was sleeping, Jude debated the idea. It was startling, different than anything she'd thought of for herself. Although having grown up in ranching country, she had always lived in town. Her time out here had been pleasant, but the idea was as daunting as it was exciting.

Chase loved her. He wanted to marry her. Jude's heart seemed to swell a little more every time she thought of marriage with him. Of her and Chase living their lives out together.

But here? He was a cop. She'd believed his career was important to him. There was a decision to be made about her own career, such as it was. There was a time when she'd had great hopes for her accounting degree.

And then there was the money. Whose was it? Who had put it in the toolshed? Jude went back in time to the few remarks her mother had made over the years about Simon Colter, and was faced with a brick wall. The truth was, unless the police laboratory came up with some evidence of ownership, she might not ever know how that cash came to be on the ranch.

But suppose the authorities decided it was hers? It was a lot of money, enough, at least, to get the ranch started.

Jude's mind wouldn't shut down. After a while she couldn't seem to lie still any longer, and she quietly slipped out of bed, found her robe and went downstairs.

It was late. The stillness was almost tangible. Jude walked through the dark first floor to the kitchen window. The dim bulb over the back door cast eerie shadows across the yard. The pile of rubble to be hauled away had grown to a small mountain. Within the debris were several old scatter rugs, worn and soiled beyond redemption.

An unusual configuration on one of the rugs caught Jude's attention, and she squinted to make it out. When she did, her fingertips rose to her smiling lips. Shorty and Biscuit were curled up together, the cat snuggled into the curve of the dog's belly.

Jude laughed softly. It was a sight to warm the coldest heart, and hers was already close to bursting with happiness.

She glanced upward, at the ceiling, as though seeing Chase through the plaster and planks. How she loved him. Until a person experienced it, no one could imagine the joy of being so connected to another human being. The two of them had gone through a lot to reach their present understanding, and undoubtedly they would face problems and trials in the future.

But looking out at Shorty and Biscuit, Jude was able to visualize a harmony that far outweighed the strife of everyday life. She smiled, because she was also able to visualize children. And more cats, and more dogs. And horses and cattle, and chickens in the newly painted and cleaned coop.

A garden. Yes, she would certainly want to raise vegetables. She suspected that when eating elsewhere, Chase depended entirely too much on red meat. A chuckle welled, because he agonized so appealingly over oatmeal and vegetarian stew.

Jude knew she was brimming with ideals right now, but if a wife didn't look after her husband's health, who would?

Contented with her decisions, she returned to the second floor and her bed.

Chase stirred and murmured drowsily, "Honey, are you still wandering?"

"I'm all through," she said softly, and snuggled into his arms.

"Bet you were downstairs after that cake," Chase teased in his sleepy voice.

Jude laughed and snuggled closer. "I was thinking about the ranch."

"Want to tell me about it?"

"Are you awake enough to listen?"

"Wide-awake," Chase said in a tone that told Jude he was anything but.

"I like your idea."

"You do?"

"You *are* awake."

"I am now." Chase sat up and switched on the lamp. "You really do like the idea of keeping the ranch and living here?"

Jude was blinking because of the light. "Can't we talk in the dark?"

"I've got to see you for this. Jude, are you sure?" Before she could answer, Chase's excitement pushed him on. "I'd like to raise Herefords. I figure we could start with a few hundred head, but this ranch will support..."

"Whoa," Jude said, sitting up herself. "Even at a hundred dollars a head, you're talking around twenty thousand dollars. Chase, we're not sure that money is mine."

Frowning at first, Chase's expression cleared. "Jude, I'm not talking about the money from the toolshed. I've got enough in the bank to stock the ranch."

"You do? But I thought... I mean, cops don't make..."

"You're right." Chase laughed. "Cops don't make get-rich salaries. But I inherited a few bucks from my folks, and it's been drawing interest for eight years. Honey, you're not marrying a rich man, but I'm not a pauper."

Jude's surprise showed all over her face, but then her eyes narrowed. "Which man is the real Chase Sutton, the down-on-his-luck cowpoke, the hard-eyed cop, or the sneaky guy with the bank account?"

Chase sat there chuckling. "You're not really mad because I turned out to have more than a broken-down pickup and a rickety horse trailer, are you?"

"And an overweight dog and a handsome horse," Jude reminded sweetly. Her eyes lit up. "Oh, you should have seen Shorty and Biscuit a few minutes ago. Chase, they were curled up on one of those old rugs I threw out, sleeping together!"

Chase reached out and snapped off the lamp, plunging the room into darkness. Jude felt him settling down and then pulling her up against him. "Biscuit and Shorty have a lot more sense than we do, sweetheart. Let's get some sleep. We can talk in the morning."

But next she felt his hand moving over her stomach and upward to her breasts. "On second thought," Chase said huskily. "Maybe there's something we need more than sleep."

Jude smiled serenely. "I couldn't agree more."

She heard her beloved chuckling in her ear a second before his mouth began a tantalizing trail to her lips.

* * * * *

Rugged and lean...and the best-looking, sweetest-talking men to be found in the entire Lone Star state!

Diana Palmer

LONG, TALL TEXANS

In July 1994, Silhouette is very proud to bring you Diana Palmer's first three LONG, TALL TEXANS. CALHOUN, JUSTIN and TYLER—the three cowboys who started the legend. Now they're back by popular demand in one classic volume—and they're ready to lasso your heart! Beautifully repackaged for this special event, this collection is sure to be a longtime keepsake!

"Diana Palmer makes a reader want to find a Texan of her own to love!"
—*Affaire de Coeur*

LONG, TALL TEXANS—the first three— reunited in this special roundup!

Available in July, wherever Silhouette books are sold.

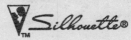

Fifty red-blooded, white-hot, true-blue hunks
from every State in the Union!

Look for MEN MADE IN AMERICA! Written by some of
our most popular authors, these stories feature fifty of the
strongest, sexiest men, each from a different state in the
union!

Two titles available every month at your favorite retail
outlet.

In July, look for:

ROCKY ROAD by Anne Stuart (Maine)
THE LOVE THING by Dixie Browning (Maryland)

In August, look for:

PROS AND CONS by Bethany Campbell (Massachusetts)
TO TAME A WOLF by Anne McAllister (Michigan)

You won't be able to resist MEN MADE IN AMERICA!

SILHOUETTE®
Desire®

Big Bad WOLFE

WOLFE WATCHING
by Joan Hohl

Undercover cop Eric Wolfe knew *everything* about divorcée Tina Kranas, from her bra size to her bedtime—without ever having spent the night with her! The lady was a suspect, and Eric had to keep a close eye on her. But since his binoculars were getting all steamed up from watching her, Eric knew it was time to start wooing her....

WOLFE WATCHING, Book 2 of Joan Hohl's devilishly sexy Big Bad Wolfe series, is coming your way in July...only from Silhouette Desire.

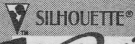

It's our 1000th Silhouette Romance, and we're celebrating!

JOIN US FOR A SPECIAL COLLECTION OF LOVE STORIES
BY AUTHORS YOU'VE LOVED FOR YEARS, AND
NEW FAVORITES YOU'VE JUST DISCOVERED.
JOIN THE CELEBRATION...

April
REGAN'S PRIDE by **Diana Palmer**
MARRY ME AGAIN by **Suzanne Carey**

May
THE BEST IS YET TO BE by **Tracy Sinclair**
CAUTION: BABY AHEAD by **Marie Ferrarella**

June
THE BACHELOR PRINCE by **Debbie Macomber**
A ROGUE'S HEART by **Laurie Paige**

July
IMPROMPTU BRIDE by **Annette Broadrick**
THE FORGOTTEN HUSBAND by **Elizabeth August**

SILHOUETTE ROMANCE...VIBRANT, FUN AND EMOTIONALLY
RICH! TAKE ANOTHER LOOK AT US! AND AS PART OF THE
CELEBRATION, READERS CAN RECEIVE A FREE GIFT!

YOU'LL FALL IN LOVE ALL OVER
AGAIN WITH
SILHOUETTE ROMANCE!

CEL1000